Gentle Fury

Dodge Merrin

eBook Edition ISBN-13: 979-8-9952599-0-9

Paperback ISBN-13: 979-8-9952599-1-6

Cover design by Mirko Fermani

<u>Content Warning:</u> *This book contains depictions of violence with some graphic descriptions of bleeding, broken bones, and other injuries.*

Contents

Chapter One

Fires Unleashed

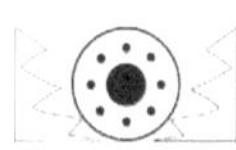

The very foundation of the stone house shook, rousing the elder warrior as falling dust coated his nearly naked form.

Instinct sent Mettius flying from his wooden bed and through the modest dwelling with sword in hand. Bare feet slapped against hard stone, but neither pain nor cold registered through his thick soles.

A single shiver drove off any remaining vestige of sleep upon encountering the night's chill as panicked shouts drew his gaze to the west. The stars illumined a cloud of dust and debris issuing forth from the ravine as leather-armored guards fled before it, and the elder's grip tightened on the sword hilt as he charged toward these men.

He locked gazes with the one in the lead, his jaw clenching when he saw the whites of the man's widened eyes, but the warrior made no attempt to look away from his old teacher.

A beam of reddish light arced down from the northern clifftop, stopping him in his tracks as it sliced through half the town, shattering rock with thundering blasts and setting ablaze a wooden cart. Horses screamed in the stables at the other end of town as people poured from their homes, shouting and looking around frantically as flaming arrows rained down from all sides.

The warning bell sounded its sharp, quick tones, snapping Mettius from his surprised stare despite being too late for its primary purpose.

"What's the matter with you! Gather the people and get them out of here!" Mettius shouted at the guards as they slid to a stop in front of him. Three more of the reddish beams joined the throngs of arrows, provoking all four of them to cover their heads as debris pelted them and dust choked the air.

"We can't," one of the six panted. He took a deep breath which only served to set him coughing from the thickening smoke and rising smell of burnt flesh.

"The ravine. It's ... blocked," another managed to gasp.

The elder looked past them and through the swirling dust and saw that the one opening through the solid rock surrounding their town was indeed filled with boulders.

"There was a flash of light and roaring thunder. The stones blew apart and came tumbling down, crushing Garrus."

A quip about how that likely improved that man's face came to mind, but Mettius brushed it aside before it had a chance to finish forming.

Another beam shot over their heads and struck one of the two guard towers near its base, and even Mettius couldn't stop himself from recoiling when the quarried stone blew into pieces. That which was meant to protect them dissolved into dozens of projectiles shooting through the air as if flung by a sling to strike down many of the panicking townsfolk.

"The gods have come to destroy us!" a warrior shouted as he glanced around at the clifftops.

Mettius backhanded the youngster across the face, not caring when he bloodied a knuckle on the chin strap as he held the man's gaze with his own.

"Get the people together and lead them up the cliff path," he growled, confident he could be heard even through all the noise.

"They control the clifftops!"

Now he grabbed the man by his armor's shoulder strap, pulled him in close, and leaned in until their noses were touching.

"We are warriors of Stoneforge, and we will fight our way through to save as many as we can, or we will die with honor and prove ourselves worthy to spend eternity with Malius," he hissed, invoking the name of the god of heroes many of the warriors considered to be their patron.

The young man set his jaw, gave his elder a quick nod, and Mettius shoved him away.

"People of Stoneforge! Take heart! Come to us!" the guard called out as he rushed into the panicking mob.

Satisfied for now, Mettius ran for the cliff path, calling every warrior he saw to follow him, and by the time he reached the thin trail leading up the face of the southern cliff, a dozen men were with him shouting their war cries. Most were in nothing but loincloths and wielding swords like Mettius, but a few of them had managed to don some of their armor and/or grab a shield at the very least.

The rough stones cut through the elder's calloused soles, but he ignored the bruising pain and tuned out the yelps of those struck by the arrows continuing to rain down upon them.

He pivoted through the first twist in the path, grit his teeth against the burning in his legs as he powered up the next stretch, then he darted around the next turn and kept going over ground turned slick with blood.

It felt like ages as the ongoing screams and shouts of his people below rang in his ears, but at last Mettius made it to the top to confront those who dared to incur the wrath of the Stoneforge Warriors.

The point of a spear greeted him at the top, striking out from the darkness toward his gut. He leaned to his left, grabbed the shaft, and pulled back, yanking the shadowy figure behind it toward him. In an instant, he spotted bright green eyes between helmet brim and mask. Releasing his grip, he elbowed the man in the back to send him screaming over the cliffside with the fires from below shining in his dark armor.

He quickly bounded off the path to the left, allowing the man behind him space to enter the fray before engaging his next target. This one had tossed aside his spear and drawn a sword which he now swung at the warrior's midsection, but it missed when Mettius sucked in his gut and bent at the waist.

A spear thrust from the right grazed his stomach, cutting deep enough to draw a fair amount of blood, but what little pain he noticed told him it was shallow enough to ignore for now.

Mettius grabbed the offending spear with his left hand, forced its owner to release it with an elbow to the face, then used the weapon to block another swing from the swordsman. With just the one hand, he twirled the spear to plant it in a patch of dirt business-end up, kicked the swordsman in the shin with the flat of his foot to avoid injuring himself, and finally elbowed him in the back of the head when he fell forward to drive him into the spear point.

Unfortunately, it failed to penetrate his armor and simply snapped in two from the weight as the soldier fell.

By now, the spearman had recovered by drawing his own sword and now thrust at Mettius' gut before he could finish off the first one. He spun to the left and slashed at the man's neck, but his sword just slid off with a metallic hiss.

Even their joint armor was strong enough to stand up to a sword strike?

Who are these people?

Every muscle in his body tensed from rage and frustration as the man turned to face him again, his blue eyes and armor shining from the fires below and stars above. The other one was almost on his feet, leaving the veteran warrior only seconds to figure something out before being outnumbered again.

"Enough!"

He charged forward as his target backstepped and held up his sword in both hands, but Mettius easily batted it aside with his off-hand and drove his own blade straight into those shining eyes.

He yanked out the blade and shoved the dead man to the ground in the same motion, then turned to face his other challenger.

The soldier's wide hazel eyes darted from Mettius to his dead comrade and back again. A single step from Mettius sent the man running for his life.

Mettius turned back toward his comrades, many of whom were now on the ground in greater numbers than their attackers, and saw that more warriors had arrived from below and were keeping the enemy soldiers at bay while townspeople ran past.

An enemy near him pulled a spear from an old man lying flat on his back, then took aim at a woman exiting the path. Before he could throw it, Mettius grabbed his forehead from behind, drew his sword across the man's face, and tossed him to the ground screaming and clutching at his eyes. He'd probably live, but would never again be a threat to anyone.

"That's all of them," a young warrior gasped after jogging up to him.

"Warriors, retreat!" Mettius croaked, his deep voice cutting through the sounds of battle despite the tightness in his throat.

Never before in his life had he considered giving that command, but there was no honor in dying needlessly.

The old man watching the scene of death and destruction below from his perch atop the eastern cliff imagined himself as being one with the night, a scarcely visible apparition come to destroy the world of mere mortals. Only his long, braided hair and beard of steely grey moved in the wind above his crossed arms with hands securely tucked into the sleeves. His blue robes melded seamlessly with the darkness as their purplish trim sparkled in the starlight to complete the semblance of an otherworldly being.

In a semi-circle behind him stood six tall, broad-shouldered men in full plate armor trimmed in purple and wearing no mask to designate them as his personal guard. Their only weapon was a sword in a leather sheath hanging from the left hip upon which rested a hand as keen eyes kept watch for any possible danger.

An army captain, designated as such by the white plume of synthetic fibers running the length of his helmet, approached from his left.

"It is over, Triume."

"How many escaped?"

"Our best estimate is that less than a quarter of the residents broke through our line, Honored One."

"How did your men perform? Were they convincing in the pretense of preventing any escape?"

"I believe so, Eminence. Many are wounded and some are dead."

"Excellent. They will tell the tale, spreading superstition and fear across all the land. Soon, they will be too weak to even consider defying us," the triume commented with a slow nod.

His next order was for the regiment to regroup for the journey home, insisting that no soldier or piece of equipment be left behind. They could leave nothing that might grant their prey any hope of standing against the forces now arrayed against them.

After the captain left, the triume lingered to look over the town, his smile growing with each passing second.

"Our time has come at last," he said softly, then finally turned and walked away.

Chapter Two

Behind The Curtain

Fresh from a bath where servants had scrubbed away every last trace of filth from the wilds outside the city, Triume Jasud Feril strolled into the debate chamber where his two counterparts already stood beside their large, black chairs in the center. The soft, red glow of the great crystal below their temple filtered into the room through immense glass windows forming the chamber's walls, reassuring him that he was home.

The junior member of the triumvirate, a man seventy years younger than himself by the name of Vejalon Cazeta, glared through narrowed eyes at Jasud as he strolled across the plush red carpet. As befit her manner, the second eldest, Yalina Leswinu, betrayed no emotion as the eldest of Zaqulon's ruling order settled into a standing position beside his chair.

"Have you no shame?" Vejalon accused, eschewing any formalities in his displeasure.

"What do you mean?" Jasud responded with a mocking grin.

"You dare to act without the knowledge or consent of the full triumvirate, then keep us waiting for an explanation," Yalina clarified.

Only a natural-born talent and nearly two centuries of experience kept Jasud from displaying any emotion as he looked over at this woman with braided snow-white hair hanging down to the small of her back. Despite her age of one-hundred twenty-eight being much less than his own at one-hundred seventy-two, this woman persisted in the habit of taking on a motherly tone as she watched him with hands folded at her waist.

All three of them bore the triumvirate's mark of power on their foreheads, a diamond-shaped brand with an equal-sided triangle inside, and were dressed in flowing robes of black and midnight blue swirled together. The only difference in their attire was in the crushed jewels sewn into the trim of their garments with amethyst for Jasud, diamonds for Yalina, and emeralds for Vejalon who was only in his sixth year of service as a triume at the age of one-hundred three.

"These warriors put our plans in jeopardy by thwarting the first phase and needed to be eliminated before we continued," Jasud argued.

"We agreed that the Naerans were sufficiently weakened by our proxies and all would proceed as planned," Vejalon countered.

"Untrue. I warned you that it would be hazardous to proceed exactly as planned and scheduled, but both of you ignored me. The nearness of the invasion's launch prompted me to act to ensure success."

"The triumvirate acts as one, or not at all. None of us should ever act alone, and that includes you!" Vejalon condemned, his voice rising.

"I'm sure that will be of immense comfort to our people as they lie starving in the streets."

"That's enough!" Yalina snapped before Vejalon could react. The gazes of the men remained locked, the dark blue of Jerald's eyes boring into the emerald sheen of Vejalon's, but both remained silent in light of their more temperate colleague's outburst.

"There is no use arguing over what has already been done. Now that you have returned, you must report on the attack and its outcome," Yalina continued.

"The town is destroyed and nearly all of its inhabitants are dead. Those who fled will tell of our great power, and their foolish superstitions will sow even greater terror among all who hear the tale," Jasud boasted.

Vejalon snorted derisively, but the older man simply ignored him.

"How many of our own people were hurt or killed?" Yalina pressed.

"None," Jasud lied with a dismissive shrug. The insistence of the others on adhering to that dated tradition of never directly interacting with the common people would prevent them from ever learning the truth, and he didn't care even if they did. His plans were too far along for anyone to threaten now.

"That will not always be the case," Vejalon intoned.

"Some must be sacrificed if all are to live."

"Much preparation remains, and no more needs to be discussed today. I suggest we adjourn to attend to our other duties," Yalina interrupted, and Jasud cast a victorious smile at his junior.

"Agreed," Vejalon growled through gritted teeth, then stormed off when Jasud nodded his consent.

"Our people look to us for guidance, and we are all committed to this path. You must have faith, Jasud," Yalina chided once they were alone.

"All that for which we have prepared for so long will soon come to pass."

The attendant closed the gate of black metal bars behind Vejalon with a reassuring click, and the triume released his tension with a long sigh as the lift activated its descent to the ground far below.

He looked through the thick glass at the city sprawled out below and completely filling the crater around the great crystal at the center, the warm red glow of which lit the surrounding area. The sun nearing its apex lit up the city from the bright blue sky above, but none of this light effectively dispelled the shadows slowly devouring this ancient metropolis.

Every structure was built from the same dark stone as made up the crater and surrounding precipices, from the towering behemoths in the northern industrial sector to the mansions in the south. Their great age showed in their faded and rain-pitted exteriors, but each was undoubtedly sturdy and bore testament to the skill of the ancient architects.

Not a single patch of green could be spotted among the aged bricks comprising the roads, nor even crawling up the sides of the buildings. Food production was moved into specialized warehouses centuries ago, and even the ground of the sports fields had been allowed to turn to dust after being repurposed for training an army, the first true military in their history of over two-thousand years.

Turning away from the city, he spent the last half of the ride facing the monolithic red-orange crystal which had birthed their civilization, closing his eyes to bask in its ever-present hum. None knew its origin, only that it fell from the sky in a time before men ever came to the region as evidenced by the immense crater surrounding it.

The first to arrive revered it as a god as they raised the first children of their great society, but later generations came to understand it wasn't alive and realized they could make use of its great power. For centuries, curved pylons placed at the cardinal directions and the web-like cage between captured its radiant energies, heating their homes and businesses and even powering marvellous devices such as a rail transportation network. Meanwhile, smaller pieces found in caves at its base and scattered around the crater were used to develop other devices for personal use such as lanterns and timepieces.

Originally founded as a priesthood of the crystal god Zaqu-ishna, the triumvirate to which Vejalon now belonged lost much of its power in that age of enlightenment, only surviving by taking advantage of a new faith that eventually arose combining the old religion and the new science. After the temple was built above the crystal, supported by the pylons, they withdrew from public life to retain their authority within an aura of mystery no one dared question.

When he opened his eyes and took in the crystal once more, Vejalon thought it appeared a little less bright than when he'd gazed up at it as a child, but in his heart knew that wasn't quite true.

Nearly a century ago, their researchers discovered the Great Crystal was dying, as so many of the smaller ones had over the millennia. It was then determined the only chance for their people's survival lay in expanding their territory to secure farmland before their own facilities failed and the time had come for the current rulers to put that plan into action.

And so they'd spent the last several decades scouting the nearby lands, wild areas into which their ancestors made few forays but now held their only hope for survival. Long studies were conducted on the peoples they found, primarily focusing on how they waged war, and all they learned was carefully implemented into their new army.

They even allowed a criminal from their first target to live with them for a time, instructing and equipping him for the purpose of wreaking havoc upon his own people. What did that say about their own values of law and justice?

Sighing again, the triume turned to face the other door as the lift neared the bottom.

No matter what they did, his people would soon be dying by the thousands, and he feared he would live to see the end of a civilization once-thought to be eternal.

The lift slowed, settled softly on the ground, then the attendant in a crisp blue uniform suit outside pulled open the gate before resuming a stiff standing position to the right. Vejalon nodded courteously as he passed and slowly headed to the south, fully capable of moving faster as a middle-aged man but needing to maintain a dignified image now that he could be seen by people other than his fellow triumes and their servants.

Anyone who saw him, from police in their black uniforms of synthetic fiber to government workers in their colored cotton robes, gazed at him with awe as they bowed and backed away to a respectful distance. The triume made sure to hold a pleasant smile as he walked, but did not acknowledge them and kept own gaze forward.

Upon finally reaching the expansive, thick-walled building of dark stone containing the city council chambers, he ascended the two dozen steps and entered through the wide-open stone doors ten times the size of even the largest man. Beneath vaulted ceilings, the wide halls were lit by wall sconces pouring forth their reddish-light from between portraits of triumes. These mystical rulers from the distant past stared down at him as he headed toward the building's center, caring nothing for the colorful tapestries or polished stone as his steps echoed in the empty spaces. All this opulence hearkened back to the days this served as a palace for the triumvirate before the commissioning of the temple and remained to awe the people but was of no consequence to one such as himself.

His polite smile faded at the sound of angry voices drifting down the hall to him from the debate chamber. He slipped inside and stood in the shadows near the door to listen for the cause of this conflict, and a frown fully took over his features upon hearing his people's current struggles.

"How are we to maintain order if you take all of our supplies?!" the head of the city's security, Warden Nelsid, demanded to know.

"This city has needs! Not everything can go to the war!" Persephora, the market district magistrate, added red-faced.

All nine members of the council were seated behind the stone table upon the dais at the far side of the room with most of them looking ready to lunge at each other's throats with the slightest provocation. Only Administrator Hirn, the council's leader, was silent as he sat there with his face in the palm of his hand.

"Victory in this war is the city's only hope for the future! Our soldiers need equipment, and I need the materials to manufacture it!" Badim, the industrial magistrate, yelled back, pounding a fist on the table to prove his point.

"There is no future if the people starve!" Persephora countered.

"And are they to do nothing but work and sleep while this is going on?" Rafik, the entertainment magistrate, added matter-of-factly.

Having heard enough, Vejalon stepped forward and nodded at the fully armored guards who responded by loudly tapping their spears on the floor. The annoyed council members glanced at the one who would dare intrude on their discussion, but all rage evaporated once they spotted the triume and they respectfully directed their gazes to the floor.

"Are we to war amongst ourselves before engaging with the savages?"

The triume's quiet challenge hung heavy in the air as he proceeded to the exact center of the room marked by a white circle, appearing to glide rather than walk thanks to his stiff robes which swept across the floor.

"Honored One, we are low on war-production materials. The other sectors are refusing to comply with the triumvirate's order to release more resources to our factories," Badim answered.

"How did this order come to you?"

"An agent relayed it, Eminence."

The triume glanced at the other magistrates who were clearly seething but also dared not risk appearing uncooperative. This was no doubt Jasud's doing, as it most certainly was not a command from the triumvirate as a whole, but despite his own objections to the man's methods, Vejalon knew they must maintain a united front with the people.

"The rest of you believe you don't have enough to spare?" he asked of the other magistrates.

"Our concern is that we are already stretched thin and must wonder how much more the people will accept giving up, Honored One," Persephora answered honestly but humbly.

"I understand. I will address these concerns with the full triumvirate. Until we issue our final ruling, I personally declare a pause on the command for the security and market sectors. Compile a full inventory with regards to what can be spared and I will send an agent for it in two days."

"Our services are also at risk of being unable to meet the needs of the people, Honored One," Rafik interjected.

"The people will not suffer needlessly should there be less theater for a time. I trust you to prioritize those options which best serve them. Be assured the rest will return in time with greater magnificence than ever before."

He concluded by looking each of them in the eye, including those who hadn't spoken, and received an affirming nod from each. Now satisfied the matter was resolved for the moment, he turned and left the room.

His task now was to share this development with Yalina and discuss their options. She wouldn't like the idea of working against one of their own any more than he did, but they couldn't allow Jasud to continue acting unilaterally.

Chapter Three

The Warrior's Burden

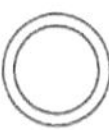

The morning prayers for this week's day of rest complete, Keid fodi Mekail stepped out of the chapel and stood beside the enormous wooden door on his right to allow the other monks in their robes of grey wool to pass by him. He crossed his arms inside their baggy sleeves and sighed contentedly with his first breath of fresh air, a welcome reprieve from the mustiness within, and looked toward the small park directly ahead where a muscular young man wearing a white tunic sat on a bench under budding trees.

His joints creaked upon descending the chapel's stone steps, but the monk paid his aging body little mind as he made his way to join his young friend, breathing deep of the air rich with flowery scents and smiling when he recognized the brooding look on Raldus' face.

"It's time we make another trip," Keid remarked as he sat down.

He waited patiently as Raldus wistfully glanced across the stone plaza at the arch in the wall surrounding the town and monastery. It had only been a few months since this young man set aside his warrior upbringing to seek a life of peace, and in moments like this Keid saw the conflict that continued to batter his friend's spirit.

"I should be here to help with planting the crops," Raldus finally sighed.

"Our people have been planting, tending, and cultivating their fields since long before you arrived. You are called to a higher purpose."

"Perhaps, but we will still need to leave before the end of the month, and Jerald doesn't seem to be in any rush to let us go," Raldus responded. Few referred to the abbot by name alone, but the young man clearly felt no need to change how he addressed the man even after converting to their faith.

"Why the rush? We have all spring and summer before us," Keid teased.

"You know why," Raldus growled in response, eliciting a triumphant smile from the monk.

"How long now until Ariela gives birth?" the older man asked next.

"Less than four months."

"We don't have to go to Naera again. There's Limurus and the fort only two day's walk from here, or we can wander the countryside visiting farmsteads," Keid suggested.

Three months ago, the two of them took their first missionary trip to the republic's capital where little more was accomplished than Keid learning more about Naeran culture and its pagan religion. After being back home for two months, he itched to get back out there and tell people about Rosjen and the eternal salvation he offered.

"That's possible," Raldus mused. The monk looked at him and frowned upon noticing his far-off gaze which had yet to change since before he sat down.

"What troubles you, my friend? Are you worried about being a father?"

"No. I don't know what it is, and that uncertainty bothers me more than anything else."

"Tell me."

The young man tensed in a manner reminiscent of the days when he would have stormed off rather than answer, but then he sighed and looked at the grass between his sandaled feet.

"The bandits are gone, the northern tribes pushed back, and even the war with Esbera is over. I should feel safe and at peace, but I don't."

"You can't think of anything that could be causing this unease?"

A simple shake of the head was all he received in response.

"That most likely means it is coming from Rosjen. He speaks to all of us in different ways, and must be using your warrior instincts to warn you of a coming need," Keid explained.

"What should I do?"

"What *are* you doing?"

The young man gave him an irritated glance before looking away over the forest beyond the stone wall surrounding the monastery and town.

"I'm training most mornings before breakfast. I want to stop, or at least not do it as often so I have more time with my wife and energy for the work, but I'm convinced I have to keep it up," Raldus explained.

"That is all you need to do for now. The task for which you are preparing will be revealed soon enough. All you can do in the meantime is to remain ready for when our Lord calls on you," Keid encouraged.

The chapel bell sounded to mark the seven o'clock hour, causing Raldus to stand and excuse himself so as to join his family in their day of rest activities.

As he watched him go, the monk wondered if his desire to reach out to the people was connected to the feelings his young friend had expressed. His heart said it was, and suddenly he knew that their lives were soon to change in ways no one ever imagined.

Beneath skies shrouded by thick clouds, the brown stallion weaved in and out of the line of barrels under the expert guidance of its rider. Raldus appeared as one with the powerful beast, moving in perfect sync as it turned and jumped, yet he also stood out due to his white tunic bound with a single belt across the waist.

Upon joining the community of Our Sacred Refuge, Raldus discovered a passion for working with the animals, particularly the horses, by incorporating what he was taught as a warrior. One of the first things he noticed was that they received little exercise since they were only occasionally used for a trip to the nearest city or to pull a plow, and at best were left to wander their pen the rest of the time.

So he decided to set aside a space between the stables, blacksmith, and houses in the northwest corner of the town. Six barrels in a slalom line and three long fences of varying heights now occupied that space. No fence surrounded this training field, leaving only the bare dirt to mark it between patches of short grass once again taking on hues of bright green.

It wasn't much, but it was enough to keep the horses healthy and his own skills sharp.

Man and beast swung around in one smooth motion and lined up with the fences.

"Yah!"

A sharp shout and spur of the heels sent the horse into a canter as the rider further leaned over its flowing mane.

They cleared the first jump with room to spare, but at the apex Raldus noticed a boy in a blue shirt, brown trousers, and simple shoes sliding to a stop at the other end of the field. He quickly leapt over the last two obstacles, then trotted up to the boy whom he now recognized as one of the helpers at the monastery.

"Is something amiss?" Raldus asked as he rubbed the sweaty neck of the panting steed.

"We have visitors. The abbot wants you to come straight away."

"I understand. Take Brutus here back to the stable for me," Raldus responded, swinging his foot shod in strapped ankle sandals over the horse's hindquarters and jumping to the ground. He handed the reins to the boy, then walked swiftly but calmly toward the compound's entrance at the south.

The soft, warm wind carried tense voices to him as he crested the stairs to the monastery complex, but they did not contain any fear or anger, so he kept to his pace as he crossed the plaza of grey stone bricks.

Near the one open arch in the wall surrounding both monastery and town huddled a dozen monks in grey robes, and from this assembly Jerald and Keid's voices rose above the frantic whispers of the others. Both men were conversing with a third whose voice he did not recognize, but the accent of which clearly belonged to Naera, the republic's capital city.

His heart skipped a beat as he realized this was most likely a messenger from the senate, and there was only one reason he could fathom for them to send someone this deep into the great forest.

"What does this mean for us?" he heard Abbot Jerald say when he reached the group. The monks noticed Raldus and spread to each side to grant him passage, revealing a man in a white tunic with a blue stripe running its length from the right shoulder to the bottom above the knee, marking him as a senate deputy. His mouth was open with a response for Jerald, but he closed it upon seeing Raldus.

In front of the man stood Jerald and Keid who followed his gaze to the warrior while the deputy's retinue of four armored guards raised their spears in salute. The visitors were all on foot; their horses likely already having been led away to be given food and water.

"What has happened?" Raldus questioned after the guards lowered their spears in response to his nod. He still had mixed feelings over receiving this level of respect, but put all of that out of his mind as the deputy stepped up and handed him a scroll tied shut with twine and sealed with red wax bearing the consul's mark.

"Raldus Velix Praelior, you are hereby summoned to meet with the consul on a matter of utmost importance. The people need their champion," the deputy announced, calling him by the full name bestowed upon him by the consul in honor of him defeating the rebel Tallio Atroni.

Raldus untied the string, broke the seal, but didn't read it and handed it to Jerald instead.

"What has happened?" he repeated.

"The town of Stoneforge was destroyed in a surprise attack nearly two weeks ago," the deputy finally answered.

Keid lay a hand on Raldus' shoulder and held his gaze when he turned to peer at him.

"By the sound of it, the warrior order is all but destroyed. I'm so sorry, my friend," the monk revealed.

Looking back at the deputy, Raldus asked him how many had survived.

"Thirty-four. Only six of them were warriors."

"Only? Are the lives of the others somehow less valuable?" Jerald interjected, having finished reading the document and now holding it at his side in his right hand.

"Yes. Warriors trained from childhood to protect the people of this land do have more value than a mix of women, children, and old men."

"Those people deserve to live as much as anyone else!" Keid berated, his voice rising and hand sliding off Raldus' shoulder.

"What of my father?" Raldus asked before the argument could continue.

The deputy stared at him wide-eyed and mouth agape while both Jerald and Keid suddenly looked at the ground. The shame expressed by the monks was harder to confirm with the elderly abbot, given his habitually hard gaze and long grey beard further hiding his features, but Raldus was getting to know him well-enough by now to read his nuances.

"My apologies, Champion. I should have already informed you that your father is well and awaits you in the city," the deputy finally revealed.

First suppressing a relieved sigh, then a derisive snort, Raldus acknowledged the news with a simple nod that betrayed no emotion. He was happy that his father yet lived, but doubted that the man had any desire to see him again, no matter what had transpired.

"Does it say anything else?" Raldus asked Jerald, pointing a finger at the document still clutched in his hand. The old man glanced at it as if he had completely forgotten about it, then told him it was nothing but an official version of what the deputy had reported.

"Rest here tonight. There should be rooms in the main building," Raldus remarked to the deputy as he turned to go.

"We should leave immediately!"

"I will not leave my wife and unborn child without speaking to her first!" Raldus shot back as he walked away.

"You must go."

Such was Ariela's conclusion as she looked into her husband's green eyes through the shroud of doubt darkening them. She'd listened in silence as the two of them stood in the front room of their home, allowing him to share the news before stating what she knew from the moment he came inside hours before the coming of dusk.

Although bleak with the threat of a rain shower, the sunlight filtering through the open windows illuminated and warmed the space enough to forgo the need for candles or a fire. Both were comfortable now, but their clothes remained heavy with the sweat of their daily labors.

"If I go, I will not be here when you give birth," he objected, placing his right hand on her rounded belly which she grasped in both of her own.

"You will be with me because I will be with you. I did not let you go alone last time and will not this time," she revealed.

"Absolutely not!" Raldus exclaimed, pulling back his hand and backing away to better stare down into her eyes.

"I can help."

"I don't doubt it, but I don't know what I will be facing. It's too dangerous."

"That's what you said last time, but I came through unharmed."

"You weren't four months pregnant, and even if you weren't with child now, I would still refuse to allow it. Anyone capable of destroying Stoneforge is far more powerful than a rabble of bandits."

"Which means that even more people are going to get hurt this time, giving greater value to my skills as a healer, not less."

He glared at her, then slowly walked over to the couch and sat down, his expression softening as he looked up at her but not showing any sign of giving in.

"My focus needs to be on the fight. I can't be distracted wondering if you are safe. If I am to do what I need to do, you need to stay here where I am sure you and the child are safe," he insisted.

She looked deep into those green eyes, saw his resolve, and understood that he would never change his mind. She touched the side of his face, he leaned into her hand, and both smiled in a way that showed more love than words ever could.

"I'll stay."

The abbot did not glance up from writing on parchment upon hearing his door swing open then close with a soft click, nor at the sound of shuffling steps approaching his desk.

"You want to go with him," Jerald fodi Arilud stated matter-of-factly.

"I also want to take one of the younger monks with us," Keid, a persistent pain in his side, disclosed in response.

The abbot finished the sentence he was writing, plunked the quill in its inkpot, then leaned back in his chair and looked over the desk at the balding monk standing before him. Candles on their stands lit his visitor from behind while sunlight coming through the colored window behind the abbot cast him in a blue and red glow.

"I'm not convinced that would be wise," Jerald confessed.

"They need to learn, and that is best done by doing."

"You and Raldus have only taken one trip together outside our walls. It would be better for you to gain more experience before attempting to teach someone else."

"Whose fault is that?" Keid remarked with a pointed gaze.

The abbot did not respond, but merely sat there watching his old rival. They had formed an uneasy friendship after being brought together by that warrior who arrived at their doorstep nearly dead two years ago, but some arguments never went away. This one had changed shape from if they should leave the safety of their walls to spread their faith to exactly how much they should interact with the outside world, and Jerald recognized the all too familiar signs of another endless argument forming.

"Are you thinking of anyone in particular?"

"Katriel fodi Yisge."

"He's still young, not any older than Raldus himself. A monk with a few more years of wisdom within him would be a better choice."

"He learned about the Naeran people from Raldus while supervising him after his initial arrival, and told me those things in turn when you would not allow me to personally speak to our guest. This makes Katriel the best choice to connect with those people now aside from Raldus himself."

This chain of knowledge was previously unknown to the abbot, and his eyes narrowed at hearing about it now.

"What did *you* learn?"

The middle-aged monk opened his mouth to speak, but closed it again as he reconsidered his answer.

"I learned that I am not immune from making assumptions," he finally admitted.

Jerald watched him for a moment, considering the changes that had come over both of them. As his people's spiritual and civic leader, he greatly desired to keep them safe from both spiritual and physical harm, but there was no denying they were already beyond the point of no return. Perhaps it was time he started putting more trust in his juniors by giving them space to move as they felt directed by their Lord Rosjen.

"Go. I will see all of you at the gate in the morning," the abbot agreed. Keid gave him a quizzical look, having most likely expected more resistance, then nodded and shuffled out of the room.

When he was gone, Jerald rose with a sigh, his joints creaking even more than the wood of the chair now relieved of its burden, and turned to peer out the stained-glass window at the town below through the center of the red circle on a blue background.

Most of his sixty-four years of life were spent guiding and protecting these people the best he could. The town and monastery built to safeguard those nearly killed for their faith had done exactly that for many decades, sheltering them from storms and wild animals while the forest hid them from those who chose violence over dialogue.

Now it appeared those stone walls and buildings were no longer enough, and their only hope lay in the strength of their faith.

"Take care of each other," Raldus told his family.

Though it was hard to see his wife, her father, and her brother in the shadows within the community's entrance arch, sheltering there from the soft rain afforded them as much time as desired to say their farewells.

"We're safe here. You worry about coming back alive," his wife's father, Imri, responded. Tobias, Ariela's younger brother, didn't say anything as befit his temperament, so Raldus just gave him a friendly smile before turning to clasp his wife about the shoulders while gazing into her hazel eyes.

"Don't push yourself too hard. There's nothing wrong with letting others take care of *you* every now and then," he admonished, savoring her annoyed yet somehow sweet smile as she looked up at him.

"Make sure you remember that as well," she shot back, drawing forth an amused smile as he pulled her into a tight embrace.

Movement to the right caught Raldus' eye, so he released her and turned to see Jerald and the two monks who insisted on traveling with him walking up with the deputy and his guards following. All of them were leading horses, and a red-shirted boy walked beside them leading one for Raldus.

"Is everyone ready?" Raldus questioned.

"Are you?" the deputy answered impatiently, but the warrior ignored him and glanced at the monks to receive affirming nods.

His next act was to look at Jerald, who then told everyone to bow their heads. Raldus noticed a quizzical expression upon the deputy's face, likely borne from confusion at seeing no nearby shrines or idols. Neither he nor any of those in his party bowed, but they kept silent as the abbot prayed to Rosjen for a quick resolution to the conflict and for everyone's safe return.

When that was finished, Raldus smiled one last time at his family, his gaze lingering on Ariela's belly before meeting with her eyes, then he turned and led his horse through the gate, mounting and nudging it into a trot after reaching the other side.

Chapter Four

The Real World

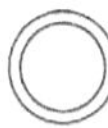

No one complained when Raldus and the senate deputy agreed to stop for the night at a roadside inn, certainly not Keid whose entire body ached after three days of travel. Even the straight Naeran roads of paved brick proved arduous for a monk of forty-five whose previous experience with physical exertion amounted to gardening and walking between monastery buildings. The last two or three hours to the capital could wait until morning.

The deputy paid for three rooms: a single unit for himself, a larger one at the end of the same hall for his guards, and the last one for Raldus and the two monks with the only one of the appropriate size being in the opposite wing. After they'd stabled their horses and stored their belongings, the deputy had dinner sent to his room while the soldiers joined the other guests in the main room. It was a pleasant enough evening, so the warrior and monks chose to take their meal at an outside table away from the din of so many voices engaged in conversation.

"Do people live like this all the time?" Katriel wondered aloud after a short silence.

"What do you mean?" Keid questioned.

"All the stories we heard on the road of people getting attacked and driven from their homes. Do they really live with the threat of such things all the time?"

"Yes," Raldus grunted between bites of bread.

All around them, insects chirped and nightbirds sang in a chorus ignorant of the troubles of mankind while the occasional wind gust carried to them the scent of hay and manure from the nearby stable. Hardly something anyone cared to smell while eating, but it did less to ruin their appetites than the drunken carousing of the other guests, and the starry night brought to them a measure of introspection.

"So many are dead, and so many others are now without homes. All of this misery on top of what the bandits already caused not that long ago. How could Rosjen allow this?" Katriel brooded as he stared into the brown broth filling the wooden bowl on the table before him.

"What he allows is for us to choose our own path in life. It is people who choose to do evil, and it is also people who choose to do good. He guides us to the good, and it is our responsibility to reveal this course to the world," Keid admonished.

"Would you rather be a mindless beast enslaved to someone else's will, or do you like being able to choose your own destiny?" Raldus challenged.

"It wouldn't bother me if it meant everybody was able to live in peace."

"You can only think that because you do not understand the nature of peace, or perhaps more accurately, that of love," Keid dissented as Raldus paused after tearing his bread and looked over the pieces in each hand to give the junior monk a disgusted look.

"Huh?" Katriel reacted, finally looking his elder in the eyes.

"Is it truly love if it is forced, or must it come from one's own choice?"

There was no response as Keid continued staring at Katriel who returned his gaze to the untouched bowl before him. Meanwhile, Raldus set the bread down and leaned back in his chair to gaze into the distance, his own half-eaten meal forgotten for now.

"I don't know what to think," Katriel finally admitted.

"You are tired from our travels. Go and rest. Then your mind and spirit will be better able to commune within yourself," Keid gently told him. The young monk nodded, then stood and walked to the inn's back door, briefly letting out the sounds of conversation through the open door before dulling them again with its closing.

"What do you think of the stories saying that these attacks are the gods themselves coming to punish us?" Raldus questioned afterward.

"You know as well as I do there is only one god, and he doesn't do such things."

"That's not what I asked."

"What do you mean?"

"These beams of light they describe sound like the same thing the man with Tallio used, so there is no denying they have power. How can mortals have power over light?"

"Are you doubting our teachings?"

The warrior let out a frustrated sigh as he leaned forward to place his forearms on the table and clasp his hands, looking down at the space between them as he responded.

"Set aside the priest for a moment and help me understand who I will soon be fighting," he declared.

The words hit Keid like a slap, pushing him back against his seat while looking wide-eyed at his friend. Raldus still didn't look up as the weight of his words sank in to reveal that Keid was acting blind toward the practical matters present in this situation, and after several seconds the monk sighed and leaned forward once again. His unseeing eyes fell upon the stables to his right as he became immersed in his thoughts.

"We see how light changes when it passes through glass and feel warmth greater than before it enters. Perhaps someone has found a way to harness and strengthen this process," he speculated.

"I've never heard of anything resembling such a method. Do your histories of your people's travels from the east mention anything of the like?"

"No. It is as strange to us as it is to you," Keid admitted with a slow shake of his head.

Both of them fell silent, their eyes toward the floor, their thoughts racing with the possible origins and nature of this awesome power. Keid could not know where the internal deliberations of his friend were leading him, but for his part, he found himself experiencing a strange sense of excitement at seeing there remained many wonders for mankind to discover and explore.

If only they didn't all end up being used to sow death and destruction.

"Rosjen guard us all," he concluded aloud.

"All truth."

Chapter Five

Desperate Times

The triumes ascended the stairs carved from a single slab of stone, Jasud in the center with Yalina on his right and Vejalon to the left, their arms crossed within the sleeves of their robes and steps in perfect unison. They emerged onto the arena's center stage, turned as one to the left, and strode to the edge to look out over the assembly of men bowing on one knee in the dirt before them.

Lights on the wall surrounding the dirt field cast a reddish glow on the dozens of Zaqulon army officers in dark armor with white-plumed helmets tucked under their right arm. For decades, what was once a sports venue open to the public had served as a training center for the new army, and it was from here their great campaign would be launched at long last.

"Rise," the three commanded in unison, and the assembly rose in a single fluid motion to gaze up at their holy leaders.

A single step brought Yalina out in front of her colleagues, granting her the space to raise both arms toward the ceiling as she kept her gaze on those men leading her people into battle.

"Commanders of the army of Zaqulon, entrusted to lead those souls called forth to save our great city. The light of Zaqu-ishna fades, and one day will no longer sustain our people. We must claim new lands of bounty if we are to live on, and after a century of preparation, this solemn duty falls to you. It saddens us to require anyone to go from the crystal's light into the savage lands outside its cradle, and the leaving weighs all the more heavy on you. Take heart, for in forsaking your home for a short time, you will save it. Such is the will of this triumvirate, and our blessing resides on all who carry out that will," she intoned, then lowered her arms and crossed them within their sleeves once more.

Before stepping back, she took a moment to study those raised faces which gazed upon her and the other triumes with awe and love. The hundreds in this stadium, and the many thousands assembled by the mountain tunnels, a little over one-hundred thousand in total, had trained for decades for this conflict and were equipped with weapons and armor far superior to any wielded by their enemy. Despite all that, many would die before it was all over, forever parted from those they knew and loved, and she would remember their faces for as long as she lived.

When she was satisfied, she stepped back into line with the others, after which Jasud stepped out from the middle to take her place.

"Many decades of tireless effort have gone into securing our future, and not all who dedicated their lives to make it possible yet live to see our victory. Their great contributions and sacrifices will not be forgotten, and all who fight now will be glorified for all eternity. All the world will know who tamed it by pouring out their own sweat and blood, fertilizing the land so civilization not only survives, but grows to ever greater heights," the oldest triume enthusiastically announced.

Yalina looked out the corner of her eye at Vejalon, careful not to turn her head in the least, and recognized an irritated glance when he did the same. They could do nothing else in response to the elder triume's habitual boasting; not in front of the people.

"It is our honor to lead this effort, working without fail to study the world beyond the crater and coordinate all aspects of this immense plot, carrying on the tradition of our predecessors. We have been with you all the way and will not leave you now. I will personally lead this army into the wilds beyond and through the battles to come," Jasud declared with a flamboyant raising of his arms at the end.

The officers cheered and pumped their left fists in the air, the sound thundering throughout the theater as Yalina clenched her jaw in an effort to keep her body still as she once again locked eyes with Vejalon whose own control proved insufficient when he did slightly turn his head to look at her more directly.

Once again, Jasud was acting without their consent and in a manner which threatened to destroy their carefully built image with the people. This time he had gone too far, a fact they would have to address once alone which Yalina communicated to Vejalon through a hard stare. His response was a nearly imperceptible nod before he once again looked forward.

Jasud basked in the applause until it abated minutes later, then lowered his arms and stepped back into line with Yalina and Vejalon, the latter of whom then strode forward to deliver his speech. His voice was strained as he spoke, enough so that Yalina feared the soldiers would notice, but they gave no sign of doing so.

"Many years have passed since the discovery of the dimming of Zaqu-ishna's light, a terrible revelation which our people have handled with considerable grace. We have asked much of you during these long decades, and you have willingly sacrificed your comfort, dreams, and even your lives to lay the foundation on which our descendants will rest. The greatest sacrifice, that of immeasurable blood, is now upon us. In this great struggle, trust that each drop of your sweat and blood, every tear you shed, buys the survival and future prosperity of our people."

He paused and looked out over the crowd and stood a little straighter upon viewing the pride and absolute trust shining forth from their faces.

"The love and respect of your families goes with you, as does that of this triumvirate. No matter what happens in the coming months, you will never be alone. On you lies our hopes and dreams, and we rest easy in the knowledge you will not fail.

"Our civilization has lasted for thousands of years, and through our efforts now, will live on for thousands more!" Vejalon finished his speech, then rejoined the line as the crowd erupted into cheers.

The triumvirate stood tall and silent as its members basked in the adoration of their people, then turned in place and strode back to the center stairs as the applause continued.

"Explain yourself!" Vejalon hissed after blocking Jasud's path the moment the three triumes were once again alone in their temple's debate chamber. The lengthy trek from the arena back to this hallowed space was an agonizing one since he was prevented from speaking his mind in view of their subjects, but now there was nothing to stop him from unleashing all the fury within him.

"You have once again acted without our consent, and exposed too much to the people," Yalina accused in a much quieter tone. She would have normally chided Vejalon for his outburst, but the fact she didn't spoke volumes about her own displeasure.

"The people aren't going to suddenly stop trusting us because one of us spends a little more time among them," Jasud responded nonchalantly as he stepped around Vejalon and walked to the western window to gaze toward the tunnels and passes where the army was already underway.

"That's what you respond to; a concern about spending too much time with the people? You defied all the laws and traditions of the triumvirate by acting alone!" Vejalon condemned as he advanced on the older man from behind.

"This is not the time for discourse! It is the time for action!" Jasud roared as he whirled around, stopping Vejalon in his tracks.

"We *are* taking action! Until now, we've been taking it together!"

"We must move quickly, and we can't do that if we're standing around here arguing while our army is fighting," Jasud growled, advancing menacingly on the younger man who did not back down.

"We act together, or not at all," Vejalon said into Jasud's face when he stopped inches from his own. He tilted his head up slightly to meet the other man's dark blue eyes, nearly entangling his dark beard with Jasud's steely grey one in the process.

"Do you intend to become the first triumes in history to solve a disagreement with violence?" Yalina's soft voice broke through, but neither of them moved until she came up, laid a hand on their chests, and gently pushed them away from each other.

"Perhaps it is wrong to send our people into war and not go with them, but we cannot all three leave the city. We must also maintain our connection with those who will remain. The only solution is for me to go with Jasud and the army while Vejalon stays here to watch over the city," she then proposed.

Neither man responded.

Each glared at the other while their female counterpart stood between them, her hands hovering inches from their chests as she looked into their eyes, first one, then the other, and back again.

Seconds turned into minutes, and one might suspect the men's defiant pride had transformed them into statues, challenging each other until the end of time.

Yet, their anger did gradually cool, and each eventually saw in the other's eyes that Yalina's idea was an acceptable compromise. At last, they communicated their agreement to her with a single nod, then Jasud walked briskly from the room and Yalina lay a reassuring hand on Vejalon's shoulder before following.

The first thing Raldus observed upon entering Naera was the hush upon the vendors and their patrons within the normally boisterous market by the west gate. All whom he saw hurriedly went about their business, speaking in little more than whispers and only when necessary. Those few who noticed the deputy's retinue on their horses spared them only the briefest of glances, preferring instead to watch the clear blue sky as if fearing to get struck down at any moment.

After the market came the temples of bright white stone draped in colorful pennants fluttering in the breeze. Songs and chants flowed from within as wispy gray smoke trailed into the air from their inner sanctums. Keid and Katriel paid special attention to the people lined up outside and weeping as monks in colored robes designating the god or goddess they served ministered to them, but Raldus and the others paid them little mind.

They climbed the stairs to the forum on its platform where the dull roar of the river below proved to be the only sound despite the hundreds of people gathered before the shrines lining the walled sides of the plaza. Many more were gathered in the center where the statue of the sky god Keslu towered over the kneeling forms outside the low, circular wall protecting the frescos to Livaria around the statue's base.

The whispered prayers of the worshippers swirled together into an indecipherable buzz as the group approached the impromptu service. Katriel's mouth hung open as he gazed up wide-eyed at the bronze image of a muscular, bearded man in a toga holding a globe above his head. Meanwhile, Keid's eyes narrowed and mouth twisted into a grim smile as he observed his young charge, being more interested in the junior monk's reaction than engaging in any further study of the statue and the nature-themed images painted on the stones around it.

"I've never seen the people so afraid. Do the gods not hear them?" the senate deputy breathed as they looked down from their mounts at the worshippers.

"Perhaps ears of stone were never capable of hearing anything," Keid pronounced.

A priest in a sky-blue robe with a green sash beside the gap in the wall around Keslu's statue shot the monk a narrow-eyed look.

The deputy noticed this and turned his own gaze to his charge with brown eyes ablaze as looked down his nose at the older man. "You would do well to watch your tongue. We tolerate your beliefs, but we will not allow you to disrespect our gods."

"The same gods you believe sent this doom upon you?"

"It may well be your blasphemy which has angered them, and I can save all of us by killing you now."

"We should determine the identity of our attackers before we do anything," Raldus interrupted. Keid nodded his approval of the compromise, but the deputy simply looked forward again as they began their descent of the eastern stairs.

In the senate plaza at the bottom with its statues and fountains, they dismounted at last and handed over the reins of their mounts to servants who led them away to see to their needs. The deputy directed Raldus and the monks to a tall building where he promised guest rooms were already reserved for them, then took his leave of them and strode off to the massive senate building to announce their arrival.

As soon as Raldus and the monks settled into their rooms and ate a small lunch, the deputy took the warrior to meet the consul. Keid insisted on coming along despite both Raldus and the deputy insisting there was no reason for him to do so, but they eventually agreed that there also wasn't a reason he couldn't come along as an observer.

The three of them walked to the consul's residence; a sprawling mansion a fair distance to the north of the senate building east of the river. Already present in the private audience chambers of the republic's top leader was the overweight consul in his traditional blue toga with purple sash, the army legate in white toga with sky-blue sash, and a heavily muscled older man in white tunic and sword on his left hip.

"Announcing Raldus Velix Praelior, Champion of the Republic, and guest," the deputy declared upon entering the room.

Previously deep in conversation, the men now turned to face the new arrivals, and Raldus locked eyes with the warrior who peered back with an all too-familiar visage of thinly veiled disappointment.

"Hope is restored," the consul gushed, but no one else appeared to share his sentiment.

"I need to know what has happened before I can do anything. The stories I've heard so far have been short on details," Raldus prompted the man whose gaze he continued to hold. The eyes of his opponent, bearing the same shade of green he saw any time he looked into a mirror, narrowed as if perceiving a challenge, but his response came quiet and simple with details of the attack on Stoneforge.

"A powerful force collapsed the entrance to the ravine in the middle of the night. I awoke to the sound of rolling thunder and rushed outside to see a cloud of dust billowing forth. Before I could determine the cause of this disturbance, a beam of light came from atop the northern cliff with the sound of splintering wood. Solid rock blasted into pieces at its touch, and anything that burns went up in flames."

"How can light cause such damage?" the consul gasped.

"Let him speak," the legate counseled, and Mettius continued as if there had been no interruption.

"Flaming arrows followed to rain down upon us as three of those beams continued to tear apart the town. One shattered a tower guarding the ravine before my very eyes."

From the corner of his eye, Raldus saw Keid glance at him in shock, but he pretended not to notice and focused on his father's words as he concluded his report.

"I led what warriors I could gather up the southern cliff path to break through and save as many as we could," Mettius explained, his expression plainly blaming his son for not being there.

"Did you see any of the attackers?" Raldus questioned, ignoring the implied accusation.

"Yes. Their armor was dark, nearly blending with the night. It was thin and light, but strong enough to deflect all my attacks."

This description of the armor further confirmed that these must be the same people as the one Raldus faced in the bandit fort, but he chose to keep this information to himself for the moment.

"There have been several smaller attacks on farmsteads, army patrols, and one against a camp of soldiers returning from Esbera," the legate, named Tullus Elvorix, interjected, causing Raldus to finally look away from his father.

"Have we learned anything else from these attacks?" he asked.

"There are always a few survivors. All of them tell of men in blue armor which resists all of our weapons. At least one of these men wields a staff with a diamond-shaped piece at its top from which shoots a reddish beam of light. A few have gotten close enough to see skin above the masks they wear, and they describe it as having the hue of polished bronze."

This description of the staff and skin tone of the invaders dispelled any remaining doubt that these were indeed the same people, so he finally revealed this to the assembly after a brief reminder of the man he'd seen with Tallio.

"These people were helping the bandits?" Mettius clarified.

Raldus confirmed this with a nod, his father's expression grew thoughtful, and he looked at the legate upon reaching a conclusion.

"Perhaps they were the true power behind the rebellion all along."

"That would explain how a simple bandit was able to challenge the army. Even with the bulk of our forces deployed against the Esberans, the remaining garrisons should have easily put down such a rabble long before it became the threat it did," the legate mused.

"It's possible these newcomers were behind the Esberan attacks as well," Mettius added.

"That has occurred to me," Raldus declared as he cast a pointed look at his father.

The elder warrior glared at him in response to the implied disrespect, but said nothing.

"People are saying this is an army of the gods," the consul chimed in.

"There is no such thing," Keid spoke up for the first time.

"What do you mean?" the consul questioned as he and the legate gazed at him astonished.

"There is only one god, and he acts to save, not kill."

The consul's face instantly changed from astonishment to pity, but the legate still looked intrigued. Meanwhile, the deputy still standing to Raldus' left rolled his eyes, having already heard this and more on the trip from the monastery, and Mettius didn't react at all except to change the subject.

"These actions are clearly intended to sow fear among us, no matter who these people may be. We must not give in to it as we find a way to fight them."

Everyone present agreed with him, including Raldus who did so with a single nod as he looked his father in the eye.

"Nothing raises the spirits of the people more than knowing a champion is fighting for them," the consul remarked with a smile.

"I agree, and have decided to share command with him. Raldus Praelior, the army will follow you to whatever end awaits us," the legate announced.

Caught off-guard, Raldus looked around the room as he decided how he felt about this. All three Naeran officials were smiling patiently, but Keid appeared concerned, and then his blood boiled upon seeing the frown on his father's face.

"I accept command, and promise to drive out these invaders," he declared without thinking, then avoided the gaze of both Mettius and Keid as he clenched his jaw to force down the heat rising to his face.

"Excellent! I shall inform the people at once!" the consul proclaimed excitedly, then he dismissed the assembly with the admonition they get to work right away.

"Be careful to remember who you are and what you left behind," Keid said to Raldus when he returned to their rooms late in the evening. He had stayed at the side of his young friend all day through one briefing, remaining silent as the warrior was updated on the status of the army and discussed strategy with its officers. Over the course of these hours, he prayed and awaited the opportunity to speak the burden upon his heart.

"I'm in no mood for a lecture," Raldus shot back as he stomped through the common area toward his private room, but the monk quickly stepped into his path and looked into his eyes when he stopped. Katriel had already retired to sleep, so the two of them were alone.

"You must stay the course."

"Don't worry about me. I'll figure it out," Raldus responded, his tone stubborn but softer than before. The monk studied him, sensing a storm of emotions in the young man but also seeing that a quiet humility yet remained in those green eyes, and finally stepped back before asking his next question.

"Have you decided on a course of action?"

The warrior sighed as the tension visibly left his bulky frame, and he rested his left hand on the back of a nearby chair to ease his fatigue as he answered.

“We don’t have enough information to decide anything, so tomorrow I’m taking the warriors back to Stoneforge to see what we can learn. I suppose you want to come with us?”

“No, Katriel and I will stay here. This will give us time to reconnect with the people I met when you and I came here and hopefully establish some long-term relationships.”

“That sounds like a good idea. I need to get some rest,” Raldus responded, then hurried into his room when Keid stepped aside.

Upon entering his own room, blowing out the candle, and lying upon the bed, Keid lay there staring at the ceiling hidden in the darkness above him. As he drifted off to sleep, he wondered which of the two of them was truly facing the most danger in the days ahead.

Chapter Six

Homecoming

Every muscle in Raldus' robust body ached; sweat dripped from his brow and drenched his tunic which long ago had turned from white to dark grey. The man on his right coughed once thanks to the dust swirling in the rays of light shining into the narrow ravine from high above, then he continued digging at the pile of stones blocking the passage in front of them. It remained an imposing obstacle even after two days of heavy labor, but the warriors would not be deterred. Their home situated in a natural basin among jagged cliffs lay on the other side and their blood burned to see it again and determine the extent of the destruction.Reaching for a stone almost half his size near the top, Raldus grunted as he pulled it free, then squinted and stepped back as a ray of sunlight fell on his face.

"It won't be long now," Raldus remarked as he dropped the stone to the side by the ravine wall. He accepted a leather flask of water and drank deeply as his replacement moved up to continue clearing the last of the stones barring the warriors from entering the town of their birth.

Legate Tullus sent a team of army engineers a day ahead of them for this task, but the damage was such that they had only finished stabilizing the area and started moving the rocks when the seven warriors arrived. After joining the effort, they all worked in hourly shifts to avoid exhausting themselves from the heavy labor. The days were growing warm and humid which made it tempting to discard their tunics as they toiled, but the bottom of this scar in the earth remained cool, so they remained dressed to prevent catching a chill from the sweat coating their skin. Their armor and weapons were carefully placed near the midway point where it was safe from damage with the rest of their gear.

None of the surviving warriors from the attack, all of whom now accompanied Raldus, fought in the previous conflict against the bandits. His father revealed that Amili was still hunting raiders in the north, but both Elder Proclus and Markus perished that fateful night, the former struck down by an arrow while assembling people to evacuate and the latter killed attempting to break through the enemy line.

"The very thing protecting our home has turned it into a tomb," Mettius mused.

The two of them had spoken very little on the journey here, both unwilling to renew their rivalry or admit fault in it, but not even pride was enough to overcome the sorrow of the moment.

Before either could speak again, the five men working moved aside to allow the lead engineer to step into the cleared space wide enough for a single man. He pressed his hands against several of the piled stones on each side, shoving against them from various angles. When none of them budged, he dusted off his hands, passed all the way through, then turned and looked at things from the other side.

He finally declared it was safe, and Mettius shoved his way forward to go first in defiance of his son's right to do so as the team's commander, but nothing was said as Raldus followed him through, raising his right arm to shield his eyes from the sudden brightness.

Nearly gagging on the rancid stench of decaying flesh after the stuffiness of the ravine, Raldus quickly covered his nose and mouth with the other hand to hold back the contents of his stomach. He'd seen many people killed in his five years as a warrior, but never before had so many been left to rot.

The smell of dirt and sweat on his hand proved enough to settle his stomach, but there was no means of stopping his eyes from watering from the sting of the fetor in the air.

When his eyes adjusted enough for him to lower his arm, he saw a pile of broken stones where the two guard towers had once stood with nothing to their shape even hinting at what once stood there. The stone fence marking the reception area was broken with the stones cast asunder in many places, but some pieces of it still stood.

He spotted his father standing atop the tower rubble and approached to find the man simply standing there with arms hanging limp at his sides. Upon coming up beside him, Raldus felt his own body grow limp, and he even dropped the hand from his mouth as the sight before him overwhelmed all his other senses.

Partially decayed bodies of men, women, and children littered the stony ground streaked with black scorch marks, or were half-buried in the jagged stone blocks flung by great force over the whole area. Not a single structure remained intact, and nothing moved except swarms of flies and the long grass in the few patches of dirt as the wind circled within the basin.

The sounds of retching from either side snapped Raldus from the trance which had taken hold, and he glanced around to see several of the warriors and engineers on their hands and knees vomiting while the rest looked on in stunned silence.

"Well, you got what you wanted," Mettius accused as he made his way down the pile.

"What's that supposed to mean?" Raldus shouted after the man now stomping his way into what used to be the town. When Mettius displayed no signs of slowing down, Raldus leapt down the remains of the tower and jogged after his father.

"You never cared what happened to us. Don't pretend you aren't happy it's all gone," Mettius barked over his shoulder.

"It was you who didn't want me around!"

"All you cared about was glory and riches!"

"Both of which I fully intended to share with the town as required by the code!"

This got the elder Velix to halt in his tracks, spinning on one heel to come face to face with his son, both pairs of green eyes locking in on the other.

"What do you know of the code, you ungrateful pup?"

"The pay of the warriors goes to the town to buy what cannot be grown or hunted."

"Never pursuing wealth and fame for themselves."

"The code does not limit how much we can earn, only *how* we earn it and that all those earnings be shared with the town," Raldus insisted, his voice rising again as the familiar argument once again brought forth all the frustration from his childhood.

Mettius ground his teeth together as he stared at his son with eyes so full of rage they appeared ready to catch fire. When he spoke again, he did so with his hand drifting toward the dagger at his waist.

"Your vow was clearly made without truly understanding it, and I should cut that tattoo off your arm for your betrayal," he threatened through clenched teeth. The tattoo in question was that of a circular shield between two jagged lines on Raldus' right forearm, a symbol granted only to warriors of the Stoneforge Order.

The sound of someone clearing their throat pierced their argument, and Raldus glanced from the corner of his eye to see one of the other warriors standing there awkwardly. He immediately returned his gaze to his father whose hand was now on the dagger's hilt and felt his own anger fading away to be replaced by deep sadness.

"What is it?" he asked.

"Primus is here."

This news was enough to cause Mettius to look at the messenger, but not to release the weapon.

"When? How?" he questioned.

"He returned home two days after the attack and got in by climbing over the stones blocking the ravine. Since then he's been scouring the area for clues about who did this. He was atop the cliff when he saw us come through the entrance and climbed down to meet us."

No one spoke as Raldus continued watching his father. When he turned to look back at him, the younger Velix met his gaze as he tilted his head toward the man's waist. Mettius looked down, then finally released his dagger.

"Take me to him," Raldus told the messenger, then gave his father one last look before following him.

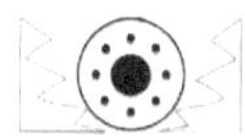

Mettius watched his son, his face hard as the ground at his feet but his mind reeling from the fact that not once during the argument did Raldus threaten or attempt violence. The boy he raised always relied on his combat skills to win fights, both physical and verbal, but now he did not recognize the man walking away from him.

The memories of every time he'd punished the child for behaving in such a manner flooded his memory, and his face grew warm at the realization of his shame. How dare he threaten violence on someone who posed no danger, much less his own son?

He shook his head to stop these thoughts and feelings from spinning out of control, then followed after Raldus and the messenger.

When he approached the two of them now in conversation with Primus whose brown leather armor stood out in contrast to the dirty tunics of the others, a group of three warriors and two soldiers nearby caught his attention and he joined them instead. All were standing beside the pool and waterfall which gushed from the rocks next to the ravine and were staring into the pristine waters.

"What are you doing?" he demanded to know, then cleared his throat from the sudden hoarseness taking hold.

"This is the only thing the attackers left untouched," a warrior commented.

"Is that significant?" a soldier questioned.

"The pool is sacred," Mettius revealed as he looked it over. Not only was the pool itself clear of contamination, but the small aqueduct constructed by their ancestors to collect the water for rituals without touching the pool or waterfall with human hands was also intact.

"This must mean that they do come from the gods," another warrior speculated.

"It means no such thing. They could have left it alone for no other reason than to have something to drink if they come this way again," Mettius refuted, then turned away and went back to his son.

"I tracked the intruders to the southeast, but lost their trail in the crags," Primus concluded his report.

"Nothing lives there," Mettius interjected.

"Can you narrow it down any more than that?" Raldus pressed.

"The best I can say is that they came from the other side of Carish Lar."

"The cursed sea?" Mettius checked, and Primus confirmed it with a nod.

The elder warrior quickly grabbed his son by the arm and pulled him back far enough to whisper in his ear and not be heard by the others.

"The Esberans believe that sea separates our world from that of the gods. Do not let the others know about this. The rumors are too strong already."

Raldus nodded his consent, then told the others to keep this quiet after Mettius let him go.

"Tesoro!" Raldus called for the officer in charge of the engineers.

"Sir?" the man said after jogging up.

"Get this man fresh supplies and assign two of your soldiers to his command," Raldus ordered the tesoro, then to Primus he said, "Rest tonight. Tomorrow, I want you to resume your search for the enemy's origin. These are mortal men, and if we find their home, we can stop them."

After the others had gone, Mettius reported to Raldus what had transpired at the pool.

"What are we going to do now?" he asked upon finishing.

"We will go north and hunt down these invaders."

Chapter Seven

No More Games

The black smoke from the stumps of trees recently felled by beam staffs hugged the ground in a thick blanket, mirroring the storm clouds blocking the morning sun and curling around the hill upon which Bujon Hannir perched as he gazed upon the fortress city in the distance. He peered over the heads of thousands of soldiers in dark armor and across the field upon which still lay the massive, burnt and smoldering trunks of the ancient woods.Soon, the mighty Zaqulon army would fill that wretched stretch of land as it marched to claim the lands explored by their ancestors long before any other human eyes ever sighted them. As their commander, Bujon finally had all he needed to fulfill the mission set to him by the Holy Triumvirate. No longer was he constrained by having to work with barbarian thugs who thought themselves strong and intelligent enough to rule this land.

That fool Tallio was supposed to be here for the invasion, acting as the Naeran king and allowing them to move freely through the land in his mistaken belief they would allow him to keep that power. The Naeran legions were also supposed to be gone, or at least weakened further than either the bandits or Esberans accomplished.

It was no matter. The republic and its army was still recovering from those attacks, and those troublesome Stoneforge warriors were gone.

There was not enough strength left in this land to stop the superior Zaqulons.

Not that they could have withstood the invasion even before the undermining efforts. The only difference was in how long it would take to fully subjugate these savages.

"The city is surrounded and all units report ready to move, Zishna," Bujon's adjutant Neqar reported, referring to him by his rank as the army's top commander, answerable only to the triumes themselves.

"Signal the attack."

The adjutant held high the staff in his right hand, a golden scepter topped with a glass globe that was half the height but twice the thickness of the beam staffs. The red light within the globe grew in intensity until it bathed all within sight in its glow, then instantly winked out, returning to its previous level.

The rhythm of thousands of footfalls in perfect sync filled the air as the army in front of Bujon began their march across the field, and his smile grew as he watched their steady progress toward the city walls.

So it begins.

"What is the meaning of this?!" Legate Tullus roared, shooting to his feet as the man who had just burst into his office dashed to the desk. A harried guard in a green cape caught up to the sweaty, panting man in leather armor and went to grab him, but the legate stopped him by raising his left hand with the palm forward.

"Merivista is under attack!" the scout enthused as he shoved a small scroll toward the legate's face.

"Explain," he demanded upon grabbing the scroll. He snatched up a knife from the tray holding his breakfast and used it to cut off the ribbon holding the parchment closed while the man caught his breath.

"An estimated twenty-thousand soldiers surrounded the city yesterday morning and are besieging it as we speak," the messenger described as Tullus unrolled the scroll to reveal a detailed account of enemy troop estimates and deployment strategy hurriedly scrawled upon its parchment.

The legate let out a string of curses under his breath as the news worsened with each new line he read.

"How did they get an army in place without us hearing about it before now?" Tullus demanded to know as he stomped out from behind his desk. Upon reaching the open door, he yelled for his assistant to send a runner to the consul requesting an emergency meeting then to have ink and parchment ready to take his orders.

"Unknown. My patrol was camped to the north of the city and was only alerted to the danger when a bright light shone from the southeast. When we realized what was happening, my tesoro sent me to report posthaste."

"You did well. Get some food and rest, then return to your turia. My orders are for you to monitor the enemy army and keep me updated as the situation develops," Tullus commanded. The messenger pounded his right fist to his heart in salute, then hurried off with the legate and guard following him as far as the assistant's desk outside the office door.

The young recruit, unarmored but equipped with a short sword at his waist, was already sitting there with a quill poised over a blank sheet of parchment. Tullus stopped there, but ordered the guard to fetch a trio of message runners before returning to his post.

He cleared his throat and stood tall so as to clearly enunciate his orders to the scribe, visualizing the placement of his troops and regional command structures as he spoke.

"To Tribune Sisenna. Deploy Wolf Legion to Fort Nelius at once."

His next thought was to send out summons calling up any remaining reserves, but remembered those few units dismissed after the recent conflicts had already been called back. It was possible form militias, but there was a reason those men weren't already in the army, and he wasn't ready to run the risk of fielding undisciplined or unhealthy peasants.

"To all cities and towns of the Naeran Republic. Any retired veterans who wish to rejoin during this crisis will be granted bonuses above and beyond their current benefits."

What about their allies in Kostrai, or auxiliaries in Esbera?

No, better leave them out of this for now. Any hint of weakness risked inflaming disloyalties and inviting fresh attacks on their borders.

"All medical units are to be informed to expect high numbers of casualties, and supply units reminded to maintain stocks of bandages and food rations."

He took a deep breath as the adjutant scribbled these orders across various sheets of parchment and pinched the bridge of his nose as he ransacked his mind for every possible need that might arise.

I'm getting real tired of these pricks appearing out of nowhere to kill my people.

"They are ready to fall," Zishna Bujon, lead officer of the glorious Zaqulon army, observed with a wicked smile as he drew his sword from its leather sheath on his left hip. Most of the other agents serving as army officers still carried their beam staffs, but he knew there would be little chance to use them once they closed with the enemy and as such chose to leave his in a safe place.

The Naeran fortress town of Merivista was indeed formidable, staunchly resisting their assault for three days no matter how many soldiers they shot from the walls or burned down in attempted counterattacks. Numerous columns of thick black smoke rose into the sky behind the thick walls, with not even the oldest of them showing any signs of abating. The trebuchets which had started those fires by flinging flaming jars of oil now sat idle behind Bujon who dared not risk causing too much damage to their prize.

After all, what good would it serve them to conquer a land teeming with wildlife and rich soil if they burned it down in the process?

In the late afternoon of the third day, the Zishna peered through his spyglass over the grassy field and viewed the remaining defenders atop the wall moving slowly or leaning on spears and knew it was time to deal the final blow.

"Signal the army to advance," Bujon commanded, then took several steps forward where his own soldiers could better see him. To his right, Neqar stepped out, lifted the horn hanging around his neck to his lips, and blew. The low, deep sound rolled across the field and reverberated off the city walls, sounding as if it rose from the very depths of the earth itself.

The sound of the horn still hung in the air when the steady beat of drums rose to take its place, and the army marched forward, their footsteps in such perfect sync that they sounded like a single creature stomping toward the city.

Fresh shouts rose from the city walls when the defenders noticed them coming, and with only a few hundred paces left to go, Bujon was close enough to see as they rushed bowmen into position who proceeded to take aim at half-draw. The command to "loose" went up, and hundreds of arrows flew toward the marching Zaqulons, but they did not react as all the unaimed shots bounced off their armor. None found purchase in the slim area where their faces were unprotected, and the army continued its steady march forward as the desperate Naerans rained volley after volley down upon them.

As they marched, Bujon kept watch for enemy horsemen, expecting to see a cloud of dust or hear pounding hoofbeats at any moment, but if any were nearby, they did not come forth. Perhaps their inability to cause any damage in the half-dozen sorties they'd run during the previous days left them preferring to hide behind their walls and archers instead.

If true, having forced the savages to abandon their favorite defense tactic bade well for the invasion and further assured its ultimate success. His confidence in an ultimate victory had never wavered, but it didn't hurt to have it confirmed.

At less than two-hundred paces to go, the arrows stopped and Bujon directed his attention back to the walls where enemy bowmen were taking careful aim as their officers calmly issued instructions in firm, but inaudible, tones.

"Now!" Bujon shouted, then ran forward at the same time Neqar sounded a short blast on his horn.

The soldiers did not shout or cheer as they surged forward, not even when the Naerans unleashed another volley upon them and many of them fell due to the nearness giving the defenders a clear shot. They only had time for the one volley before the attackers reached the base of the wall where their own crossbowmen took a knee and shot back. This forced the defenders into cover, granting the ladder teams enough space to launch the grapples from their bulkier crossbow-like devices.

Ropes spun through tensioned pulleys with a terrible screech as the hooks flew through the air, then clattered to the top and settled against the raised bricks with the ladders flopping against the wall. Within seconds, those flexible yet sturdy contraptions of cord and wood were swarming with blue-armored soldiers making their way to the top where steel-armored savages hacked futilely at the metal-covered ropes behind the hooks.

It would have been no trouble to blast holes in these primitive walls from a distance, which would have made entering the city much easier, but the triumes had issued orders for the city to be taken as intact as possible. They wanted to control this land, not destroy it, and they would move much faster by making use of the existing infrastructure no matter how inferior it may be to what they would eventually build themselves.

The soldiers in their blue armor swarmed up the walls, moving so quickly as if they weren't wearing armor at all. Bujon was at the head of his detachment, and the first thing he saw upon poking his head over the top was a spear coming right at his face. He ducked back down in time to avoid getting impaled, then grabbed the weapon when it appeared above him and pulled back, yanking both it and its owner off the wall to fall into the mass of his troops still on the ground.

He quickly scrambled up the rest of the way before anyone replaced the spearman, then snatched his sword from its sheath and swept aside a sword thrust aimed at his gut. He held the sword in one hand and used it to hold his opponent's weapon aside as he delivered a backhand strike to the man's face, his armored glove protecting his flesh from the man's leather helmet.

This knocked the enemy soldier off-balance long enough for Bujon to finish him off with a downward stab to the side of his neck, bypassing his shiny metal armor.

The Zishna spun around, anticipating an attack from behind, but instead was treated to the sight of several of his own soldiers dueling the most obstinate of the defenders. When more Zaqulons arrived, they rushed past their officer to confront any remaining Naerans on that side of him and were soon linking up with their comrades mounting the wall further down.

A crackling sound tore through the air, and Bujon looked to the north in time to watch the beam from a staff firing into the city from that wall, likely targeting Naeran reinforcements.

The walls were now in Zaqulon hands, and the army pushed into the city as both soldiers and civilians fled before them, impervious to the screams as they slaughtered all they encountered.

Their time had indeed come at last.

"Such is to be our legacy," Triume Yalina commented somberly as she and Jasud passed through Merivista's eastern gate.

Ten agents, five from each of their personal guards, marched in a square around them, their eyes in constant motion as they peered into every corner and opening. Since Jasud's lead agent had yet to return from leading the seizure of this fortress town dominating the republic's southern region, this retinue was led by Avlana, the blue-eyed, red-haired commander of Yalina's agency.

The early afternoon sun shone brightly overhead, not to be obscured by the tendrils of black smoke still swirling above the buildings, adding an eerily peaceful ambiance to the scenes of destruction around them. Even in the midst of these remains of battle, part of her could not stop thinking about the sweat soaking into her underclothes and pouring down her face in the hot, thick air while cursing this breach of protocol. How were they supposed to maintain their godlike image with the people while drowning in their own bodily fluids?

"Yes, our people will be forever indebted to us for what we are achieving here," Jasud stated proudly as he looked around. She spared him a brief glance and spotted a satisfied smirk between his steel-grey mustache and short beard, his dark blue eyes shining while he took in the sights of the city, the first either of them had ever seen outside of their own.

Upon returning her attention to their surroundings, Yalina didn't see anything worth smiling about. Burnt and broken bodies of people and animals, both of which were scarcely recognizable as such, still littered the streets from yesterday's battle. Many of the buildings were nothing but scorched blocks of clay and stone beyond any hope of identifying their purpose. Among the rubble clogging the streets were dozens of bloodied limbs sticking out, all movement having ceased long ago.

"Not even we can yet know how much this is going to cost us," she mused as a pair of soldiers rushed past bearing one of their comrades on a cloth stretcher.

"We do know the cost of doing nothing," Jasud retorted.

Their path took them to an open square where they came upon more of their soldiers stacking the bodies of the city's inhabitants. Her gaze lingered on the limp forms as an unexpected anomaly tickled at her mind, then a tiny hand flopped out of a diminutive bundle carelessly tossed onto the pile. No amount of discipline could have prevented the stumbling misstep that followed and drew her agents closer, but they withdrew again at a slight nod from her while Jasud mercifully continued on without noticing.

Now Yalina discerned that remarkably little of the burnt attire was not the armor of soldiers, but the remains of dresses and tunics. What shape remained to the broken bodies was not that of muscular frames but was instead delicate or small.

Not in front of our people, Yalina chastised herself as tears threatened to well up in her eyes.

"It was agreed long ago that the only way to claim the natural resources of this land would be by destroying all the people in it. Perhaps we were wrong to think this and have passed beyond any manner of virtue," she suggested as they paused to watch the scene.

"Not at all. This is the only way our people will survive," Jasud argued.

She did not press the point, knowing it would fall on deaf ears, but continued wondering in her own mind how their people would be forever changed by this experience, and if they would still be themselves after it was finished.

"Nothing," Raldus sighed as he stood and brushed the dust off his leather leg-guard from where he had been kneeling on it.

"These cowards can't run and hide forever," Mettius added as he looked around at the lengthening shadows.

"What if one of their powers is making it so they can't be tracked?" one of the other warriors, a boy younger than Raldus, suggested. Raldus sighed and kept looking around at the trees, long ago wearied from the debate about the nature of this new enemy and the speculation of their godhood, but the other warriors quickly stepped away from the young man. The soldiers took their cue from them just in time to distance themselves as Mettius whirled around and advanced on the poor lad until they were face-to-face.

"What are you?"

"I don't–"

"What have you trained your entire life to be?"

"A warrior."

"Of?"

"Stoneforge?"

The elder warrior glared at his junior, his jaw clenched as he fought to hold back the emotions that the answer evoked.

"Say that again," he finally commanded in a tone so low as to be nearly imperceptible.

"Stoneforge," the boy restated in a surer tone.

"Is there any challenge we will not face?"

"No."

"Do we *ever* give in to fear?"

"No!"

"I don't want to hear anything more about these people potentially having abilities beyond our own. We caught up to them once, and we will do so again. If they have something we've never seen before, we will determine how to defeat it and emerge victorious. Do you understand?"

"Yes, Elder!"

Raldus looked over at them, feeling a mixture of empathy for the boy and satisfaction at his being corrected. Some of the others looked at him as if expecting him to say something, but all he did was give them a simple nod as his father continued to stare into the boy's eyes to ensure he'd made his point.

"Someone's coming," a warrior quietly interjected, and all sixteen of them instantly formed into a circle with Raldus and Mettius in the center, all of them pulling out their swords with a soft hiss of metal on wood.

In the ensuing silence, broken only by the insects striking up their nightly chorus, they heard the steady footfalls of at least three men walking through the brush and headed in their general direction. It was obvious they weren't trying to be stealthy, so Raldus decided it was worth the risk to call out to them.

"Who goes there?"

The footsteps stopped with the travelers still out of sight in the growing darkness among the trees, then the reply came.

"I bear a message for Raldus Velix, Champion of the Republic."

"Approach," Raldus responded, but kept his guard up.

The footsteps resumed, slower this time, and soon three soldiers in leather armor emerged from the shadows. Once he was sure they were who they said they were, Raldus sheathed his sword and the others followed suit.

"What news do you bring?" Mettius questioned on his son's behalf.

"Merivista came under siege by a large army four days ago. The descriptions of the attacking soldiers match those of the ones who attacked Stoneforge," the relatively short man in the middle reported.

"Then the ones here are nothing but a distraction," Mettius observed, clutching the hilt of his sword still in its sheath until his skin visibly reddened and knuckles whitened.

"Is there any word of other armies?" Raldus questioned, ignoring his father's outburst.

"No, but we didn't even know about this one until after it had surrounded the city."

The men with Raldus began whispering among themselves as he considered the news and his options. He was getting tired of reacting instead of acting, but there was little more he could do until they had more information.

"The legate has surely dispatched a legion to the city by now. I will go and meet it," he told the messenger, then turned to his party to issue his orders. "Two warriors will stay here with the soldiers to find and destroy the enemy operating in this area. The rest are to come with me."

"I will stay and lead this group," Mettius volunteered, and Raldus nodded his approval, repeating the gesture when another warrior offered to stay behind.

With that settled, he sent the messenger and his guards back to the city, then set off at a rapid pace to the south. They would walk through the night, resting only as needed, hopefully reaching Asturios by morning where they would resupply and get some horses so as to reach the battlefield as quickly as possible.

Chapter Eight

Battle Lines

Morning fog rising at the intersection of the republic's two largest rivers veiled the land ahead of the five warriors as they trotted down the road on their steeds. A wide, dark shadow formed in the mist ahead of them, causing the leather-armored men to pull back on the reins and slow their mounts to a walk, soothing their tired mounts with whispered words in response to their snorts and whinnies.The shadow resolved itself into the grey walls of Fort Nelius as the warriors crossed the arched bridge connecting the main road to the smaller one servicing the fort while behind them the last vestiges of the nearby town of Aquabivium faded from sight.

When a messenger intercepted them on the road from Asturios to report that Merivista was already lost, Raldus set off instead for the nearest garrison to that doomed city to rendezvous with other reinforcements and stage their counterattack.

The guards at the main gate passed the warriors through without incident, and Raldus rode straight for the fort commander's office while the others headed for the barracks to receive their assignments working alongside the legionnaires. Upon entering the room lit with flickering candles to supplement the pale sunlight from the single window, the first person he saw was Legate Tullus seated behind the desk holding his head in both hands as he stared at a map of the fort and surrounding area. Leaning with both hands on the desk and also studying the map was the commander of Fort Nelius, Tribune Lucius. Both men wore segmented breastplates along with leather greaves, bracers, and belts, but their plumed helmets were currently perched on opposite corners of the desk. The horsehair combs on top of the helmets were both light blue, but the tribune's was arranged along the length from front to back while the other was fanned out to denote the legate's higher rank.

They looked up at the sound of Raldus' entry, but before any of them could speak, the lead officer of Wolf Legion, Tribune Sisenna, came in behind the warrior. Sisenna and his men were normally garrisoned at Fort Custonum near the great forest but had been called in to operate in the field while Pike Legion saw to the needs of Fort Nelius.

"Excellent timing. Tribune Sisenna, I am placing you and your legion under the command of Champion Raldus for the duration of this engagement," Tullus revealed.

"I am fully capable of administering my own legion, Legate," Sisenna protested as he glowered at Raldus from the corner of his eye.

"I never said that you weren't," Tullus scowled as he lowered his hands to lie flat on the desk and sat straighter to better meet his subordinate's gaze. The tribune chewed on the inside of his cheek, but didn't say anything and merely acknowledged the order with a nod.

"What is the current situation?" Raldus changed the subject.

The legate nodded at Sisenna, who cut short a frustrated sigh, then delivered his report without making eye contact with any of them, not even Lucius, who thus far had only watched the scene unfolding before him with mild interest.

"The enemy vanguard has secured control of the southern road, and the main body of their army is setting up camp alongside. Their skirmishers continue to attack any of our people in the area, killing all those who are not smart or quick enough to flee."

"They move fast," Raldus marveled under his breath.

"Too fast," Tullus muttered.

"Precisely. We should attack them now before they can fortify their position," Sisenna blurted out.

"We should not underestimate them."

"The champion is right. If another foe behaved this way, I would crush them beneath the weight of their own arrogance, but in this case we do not know if that ego is justified," Tullus added.

"Then what are we to do?" Sisenna scoffed.

"If Nelius falls, there will be nothing between them and Naera," Lucius cautioned.

"That cannot be allowed to happen," Tullus declared.

"We outnumber them two-to-one and can drive them back with a forward assault," Sisenna insisted.

"That's the last thing we should do," Raldus argued.

"Why is that?" Sisenna sneered.

"Merivista should have held out far longer than it did. The scouts who observed the siege report that only a few dozen of the attackers were hurt or killed, and they're not even sure about that number. We should assume we are at a disadvantage no matter how things may appear."

"Most of my men are hardened veterans from last year's war in Esbera, while the garrison at Merivista hasn't faced anything but Mortuns in decades."

There was no denying he had a point there. Although a mere shadow of their former selves, the Esberans were an advanced culture and a formidable enemy when they weren't bickering amongst themselves. The practically sub-human inhabitants of the southern swamps, colloquially known as Mortuns, or the living dead, were little more than a minor nuisance in comparison.

"Stoneforge warriors have fought everything under the sun across all the known lands, from wild beasts to full armies of men, for centuries, yet these people nearly destroyed the entire order with little trouble. We are to them as the Mortuns are to us," Raldus shot back.

"I agree with the champion," Tullus spoke up, interrupting Sisenna whose mouth was already half-open.

"We've already discussed this, Legate, and we agreed that it is unwise to let them make the first move," Lucius objected.

"No, I said that we would discuss it later. Is it not obvious to everyone by now that conventional tactics will not serve us against this foe?" Tullus countered harshly.

The two tribunes inhaled sharply and pulled back at the chastisement while Raldus bit the inside of his lip to keep from smiling. Any pleasure he felt at seeing them humbled faded upon remembering that it wasn't too long ago where he'd been far more arrogant than either of these men. When it came down to it, he didn't wish the lesson he learned through a near brush with death upon anyone.

"We will make them come to us where our numbers provide an even greater advantage behind walls and ditches. Prepare your men accordingly," Tullus concluded as he looked back at his map, signaling the conversation was over.

For days, as the invaders drew closer to his position, Legate Tullus had been unable to purge from his mind the image of a hostile army marching up the road, determined to destroy their beloved capital. He could stand it no longer and now stood at the bridge to the southern road with Tribune Lucius and an engineer to discuss their options should the battle go ill.

"How quickly can you destroy this bridge?" he asked of the engineer as they peered at the stone walkway arching over the rapidly flowing water.

"It would take several hours at least."

"The only way to prevent the enemy from using it would be to destroy it now," Lucius commented.

"No. There isn't enough room between the river and the fort for the legion to maneuver, and boats are too slow for a retreat," Tullus told the tribune, then to the engineer he instructed, "You need to find a way to collapse it under battle conditions."

The short, squinty-eyed man took a deep breath and ran his hand through his light hair, staring at the imposing structure as he considered what to say next.

"It would take many men on both sides chipping away at it with pickaxes to collapse it. There's no other way to do it," he eventually admitted.

"Find a way, unless you want to explain to the senate why an army is standing at their door," Tullus commanded, then turned away with a flourish of his blue cape and started back to the fort, leaving the engineer anxiously standing there as Lucius jogged to catch up to his superior.

Feeling no concern whatsoever, Raldus stood in front of the ditches and palisade protecting his legion and stared at the enemy soldiers who had moved further up the road during the day.These people for whom they still had no name stood in formation at the outside range of Naeran warbows as if daring them to attack. They hadn't even bothered to dig any ditches or erect palisades.

It was obvious they had no intent of making their own move, and this was his first chance to get a proper look at the invaders, so Raldus defiantly stood there studying them. In anticipation of the coming battle, he'd donned the armor given to him by Abbot Jerald who had revealed it was blessed and consecrated by the monks once a year since they received it. Although he didn't believe it held any sort of magic power, it did comfort him as a reminder of his new faith in Rosjen which held considerable power all on its own.

As he watched the invaders, tall and imposing in their dark armor with covered faces, Raldus heard someone walk up from behind to stand beside him but did not react to the new presence.

"The legate is talking about taking apart the bridge, and neither of you wants to attack and drive out these invaders. Why don't we just get the senate to go ahead and *give* them the southern region?" Tribune Sisenna mocked.

"Where do you think they come from?" Raldus asked as his way of ignoring the insult.

"I have no idea," Sisenna snapped.

"I almost died two years ago," Raldus changed the subject.

"What are you talking about?"

"I went after a bounty alone, and was ambushed by over a dozen men. I'd never lost a fight in my entire life and thought I never would. I was wrong."

"Now you're too afraid to fight. This must be why most have to die to earn the title of Champion."

This brought forth a sigh from Raldus, a long, slow exhalation borne from the depths of his soul after which he turned to look the tribune in his brown eyes.

"I learned to respect my opponent so that my own ego doesn't get even more people killed," he concluded, then walked away without waiting for a response.

"We received a message. That's why I came to find you," Sisenna called out, stopping the warrior in his tracks. He turned to look back at the man in his segmented armor and helmet with green plume running from front to back, but did not say anything and merely looked at him, unwilling to dignify him with a response after his earlier insults.

"Your father caught up with the group he was pursuing and has trapped them between the mountains and Asturios. He expects to defeat them soon."

Raldus acknowledged the news with a nod, then resumed walking away.

Chapter Nine

Face of the Enemy

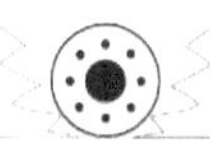

Even at this late hour, sweat clung to the skin beneath Mettius' leather armor and dripped from his brow as he crept toward the soft red glow at the base of the mountain. Nine soldiers followed him, all of them crouched to nearly the same height as the sparse patches of long grass amid the stones. Unseen opposite them, another Stoneforge warrior by the name of Brutus led nine more Republic soldiers toward the enemy camp.

For over two months these curs had pillaged the countryside, eluding any and all patrols the Naerans sent against them. Once engaged in the pursuit, even the warriors only managed to catch up with them on a single occasion, but failed to prevent their escape. After all of that, Mettius finally had them in his sights once more, and he would not allow them to get away again.

A silent grimace crossed his face as the elder warrior crouched down, his aged joints protesting but his discipline holding firm as he conducted a final observation of the camp.

The source of the light was out of view, but whatever it was made the area bright enough for him to see clearly, so he didn't have to wait for his eyes to adjust. What he saw was one man standing guard at the center front while eleven others slumbered on the open ground behind him, all of whom still wore their armor.

Was posting only a single guard arrogance or confidence?

It was time to find out.

Mettius lifted his javelin into a throwing position over his shoulder and sensed the soldiers do the same behind him. Brutus should also be ready by now and would attack when he did.

He paused a moment to check his aim, then rapidly stood and launched the projectile which was halfway to its target when the others flew over his head.

His javelin struck the guard in the side just in front of his left arm, but merely bounced off with a loud clang and fell to the dirt. All the impact accomplished was to push the man back a step. Two of the other spears missed their targets completely, their tips finding purchase in the soft dirt with shafts angling upward, while those that did strike the sleepers were deflected and fell to the ground—useless.

The guard drew his sword as ten more javelins sped toward them from the other direction, again doing nothing but bouncing off their intended victims and knocking them off balance as they clambered to their feet.

"Now!" Mettius shouted as he drew his sword and charged in. The soldiers shouted a battle cry as they followed, and the others also appeared running in from the opposite direction.

Mettius met up with the camp guard first. He feinted a left jab at the man's masked face, then thrust his sword into his gut when he leaned back, but all the attack did was push him back several paces.

Not wasting any time being surprised, Mettius unleashed a flurry of attacks on his opponent which kept him from bringing his own weapon into play, but none of them penetrated the armor. He thought about going for the face again, but was too close to get a proper angle for a killing blow. Even if it were possible, even in the midst of a fight he knew they couldn't rely on a single weakness if they were to have any chance of defeating these people.

The alien sensations of fear and doubt crept into his mind as he grew tired from the constant aggressive motion, but this only served to stoke his rage.

"Yaah!" he cried out as he drove his left fist into his opponent's face, bloodying his knuckles on the helmet brim.

The force of the blow flung the man's head back, and when his torso followed, Mettius spotted a line of skin showing at his waist. Before the guy could step back and straighten up, the warrior thrust his sword into the gap and upwards into his chest.

"Stab at the waist!" the warrior shouted as he shoved his dead opponent to the ground.

Whirling around, he spotted an enemy with his back to him pushing forward against a legionnaire who was desperately blocking the attacks. Mettius leapt toward him, grabbed the enemy soldier's forehead from behind and pulled back to expose his neck and drew his sword across it, but met only with metal.

His victim attempted to squirm free, but the legionnaire he'd been attacking stabbed him through the waist before he could wrest himself from the warrior's iron grip. Mettius then let him fall to the ground where he doubled up and groaned in pain.

Another enemy came from the side to stab the legionnaire through the armpit, after which the warrior rushed forward and stabbed him in the neck, this time getting through the thin armor protecting it.

"Stab, don't slash!" he updated as both men fell to the ground.

Now armed with the information they needed to have a fighting chance, Brutus and Mettius formed a line with the five remaining Naeran soldiers and pushed their enemy toward the slope, cutting many of them down as they went.

"We did it," Brutus gasped as Mettius yanked his sword out of the neck of the last enemy soldier from where he'd knocked him to the ground.

Neither sheathed his sword, taking a moment to catch their breath as they took in the results of their attacks, discovering that the two of them were the only ones still standing.

"Check them," Mettius commanded hoarsely.

They made their way around the camp, listening for any groans and watching for signs of movement from the bodies strewn about the ground. Upon finding neither, they knelt at each one to check for signs of breathing but confirmed that they were all dead.

"Did any of them even consider surrendering?" Brutus questioned as he stood up from the last one.

Instead of wasting effort speculating on that which had no answer, Mettius utilized the nearby bedroll to clean the blood from his sword. When he noticed the blood pooling on the skinned knuckles of his left hand, he cut a strip of clean cloth from the bedroll before sheathing the sword and standing up to glance around the camp.

"What is that?" he demanded with a lift of his chin, using it to point at the light in the center of the camp while he wrapped the cloth around the wounded section of his hand. The younger warrior followed his gaze, then strode over to the small, glowing red dome and knelt over it.

"It's warm, but not too hot to touch," he remarked as he picked up.

So these people had the power to command light not only to destroy, but also to illuminate without imparting warmth or any obvious source of fuel. What other wonders did they possess?

"We'll take it with us. Perhaps the engineers can make sense of it," Mettius grunted, then knelt and picked up one of the enemy swords.

"What does this look like to you?" he asked as he held it up.

"A spatha," Brutus answered after stepping closer for a better examination, referring to the style of short sword favored by the army.

"Have you ever seen anyone else using swords like this?"

Brutus was nearly ten years younger than Mettius, but had spent his fair share of time traveling other lands, even traveling farther than the elder warrior who was in the field for only a few years before switching his focus to training and mentoring the following generations. This was a necessary change to allow him to raise his son after his wife died in childbirth, but quickly grew into a passion for him.

For whatever reason, his lessons were not well-received by his own son, who unfortunately nearly had to die before learning to properly respect his own strength and that of others.

"No. Our weapons are based on those our ancestors brought with them after fleeing the destruction of Tresca. People in that area probably still use something similar, but everyone around here has their own cultural style," Brutus explained.

"That's what I thought," Mettius commented as he brought the sword down to hold it by his side. He knelt down again by the nearest corpse to study the armor, peering at it closely and feeling it with his free hand.

"What is it?" Brutus asked after Mettius stood again to look around, frowning.

"The underarmor is unlike anything I've ever seen, but the style of the breastplate has a certain familiarity to it, even with the strange metal and blue dye," Mettius confessed after walking up to one of the Naeran soldiers to peer at his armor.

"You think these people copied the army's equipment?"

"I don't know, and we're not going to find out anything by standing around here. I'll gather all of it together while you make something we can use to carry it," Mettius responded with a sudden burst of energy. It would be difficult for the two of them to carry so much alone without horses, but he wasn't about to leave any of it behind, even if that meant they had to drag it behind them on a makeshift sled. They might not be able to learn anything about these people from their equipment, or how to fashion the materials for themselves, but they could still use these pieces to even the odds in upcoming engagements.

"What about the dead?"

"We'll line up our soldiers and cover them with something, but there isn't enough time to bury them."

Mettius was already working on removing the armguards of the first enemy soldier, but he paused and looked up when he noticed that Brutus wasn't moving. He started to bark a command at him to get moving, but caught himself just in time and chose to speak calmly instead.

"We need to let the others know what we've learned and put this equipment to use in stopping this invasion as soon as possible."

The younger warrior hesitated another moment as he looked at the unmoving figures of those beside whom he had just fought, but then he nodded and hustled into the trees to find material with which to make a pallet.

As he got back to work, Mettius reassured himself with the fact that if nothing else, they learned at least one thing here.

These people could be defeated.

Chapter Ten

Juggernaut

There was no hesitation in Triume Jasud's stride and no doubt in his heart as he marched out in front of his army, remaining careful not to trip on his own robes of dark blue with amethyst trim as they dragged across the grass. When he reached the center of the Zaqulon front line, he stopped and turned to face the thousands of Naeran legionnaires assembled between them and the river, folding his arms behind his long grey beard as he peered at the fools in their shining armor.

It was traditional for the triumvirate to maintain a certain distance from their people, a fact of which Triume Yalina had once again reminded him as she insisted upon remaining in the rear of the army, but Jasud understood that the time had come for them to step out into the light and assert their leadership for all to see. He did not fear these savages and was ready for everyone to know it.

The sun glinted off his golden staff with the diamond structure at its tip as he angled it toward the enemy, a sight which caused many of the young legionnaires to take a step back before getting shoved back into place amid shouts from their officers. He nearly smiled at the spectacle, but suppressed the expression and maintained a sober facade. It would not do to break from all decorum.

When he squeezed the slight bulge at the staff's balance point, a reddish beam shot out over the heads of the legion to strike the wall of the fort on the other side of the muddy river far beyond the range of any bow or siege machine. Thunder split the air and the ground shook as the stone burst into a cloud of dust from which those tiny figures atop the wall not caught in the explosion fled in either direction.

Satisfied at the sense of pure terror rising from those foolish enough to oppose them, the triume lowered his staff, turned in place, then gave Zishna Bujon a dispassionate glance before strolling into the formation. As he walked, something caught his attention from the corner of his eye and he looked at the head of his staff to see that the red crystal within the glass diamond was noticeably dimmer.

For many centuries the triumes and their agents had wielded these weapons, but rarely found cause to use them in all that time. Now that they were at war, it appeared they were losing power even faster than the crystaleer had predicted.

No matter. These savages will fall before us long before we face any disadvantage, he reassured himself as he looked forward again.

"Steady!" Raldus reassured his troops. Officers repeated the word down the line, prompting raw recruits and hardened veterans alike to stiffen up and tighten their grip on javelin and shield as the last echo of thunder faded away and the roar of the river drowned out the sound of falling debris.

"Why do they not use those weapons to destroy us without engaging in battle?" Tribune Sisenna mused from the champion's right side.

"They do not fear us," Raldus remarked.

"Yet they put forth the effort to make *us* fear *them*. Why don't they just finish us?"

"Why are they doing any of this? We still know nothing about their intentions or methods," Raldus concluded.

If the tribune had any further questions, they were cut short by a horn call from the invaders and their formation going on the march.

"Archers, ready!"

Though he could not see them at the rear of his own army, Raldus pictured the hundreds of archers on the riverbank pulling their bows to half-draw.

Despite calls to make them into a personal guard, the other Stoneforge warriors were not with the legion or in the fort and were instead in the field scouting for weaknesses in the attacking force and exploiting them if possible.

"Archers, loose!" Raldus commanded.

Hundreds of arrows flew over the formation from behind, briefly shading them as though a thin cloud was passing over the sun, then arced down toward the advancing invaders who did not react as the arrows bounced off their armor.

Raldus then ordered the archers to loose at will, hoping at least some of their shots would find weak spots, but it was no use. They might as well be throwing sticks at them.

At his order, the trumpeter on his left sounded a series of three notes: one long, one short, one long; signaling the cavalry to charge. The horses thundered past them on either side, their riders gripping the reins in their left hand while holding a spear high in the right.

This time, the invaders did stop and tightened up. They ducked their heads to hide their faces as the cavalry raced around them launching their spears into the mass, but even these large weapons thrown by strong arms did nothing but bounce off their targets.

"They can't be killed!" someone behind Raldus cried out.

"Silence!" Sisenna chastised.

Seconds after the last spear was thrown, dozens of invaders rose up at the center of their formation to point strange weapons at the horsemen, the shape of which Raldus couldn't make out at this distance. They let loose with a loud twang and clunk reminiscent of the mechanism on a ballista and riders began falling from their mounts.

"Get them out of there!" Raldus shouted, taking a step forward as if to go and pull them to safety on his own.

The trumpeter sounded the cavalry retreat, a single high note, and they raced back to the formation even as a second volley bore dozens more to the ground.

"Artillery!" Raldus shouted when the invaders broke from their protective huddle and resumed marching.

The first volley of stones lobbed by catapults and ballista bolts tore into the advancing soldiers, tossing them into the air or driving them to the ground.

"Finally," Sisenna muttered when the majority of those who fell did not get back up.

Then a deep horn sounded a long blast from the invader's rear position, and the soldiers abandoned their march in exchange for a full run toward the Naerans.

"For home and family!" Raldus shouted as he drew his sword. The legion responded with a collective roar, then they all surged forward as one to meet their attackers head-on.

"For every one of our soldiers they stop, many more of them die, yet they continue to fight," Triume Yalina observed in a tone of voice approaching a sense of awe.

The thousands of men battling each other appeared as a single, roiling mass to the two triumes on a hill overlooking the battlefield next to their camp, but the fierceness exhibited by both sides was plainly visible to them and their agents.

"All that matters is that they die," Jasud commented snidely.

"There is nothing preventing us from admiring them even as we do what we must."

This statement provoked a derisive snort from her comrade, who then said, "They are primitive savages incapable of understanding that they are already beaten. Why should we spare them so much as a second thought?"

"Do not forget how much we learned from them in this quest to save our people. Our army would not exist if not for those lessons."

"Nonsense. One way or another, we would have learned what is necessary to take what is rightfully ours."

Yalina suppressed a sigh and chose not to respond out of the knowledge it was of no use. Even if she were interested in arguing with him, a new development in the battle drew the attention of everyone on that hill.

Bones cracked and snapped when the metal boss of Raldus' tower shield impacted his opponent's face, forcing the man several steps back.

The invader dropped his sword as he leaned forward to claw at his mask, but Raldus struck him in the back of the head with his sword hilt and sent him sprawling to the ground before he could remove it.

This one was out of the fight for now, so the champion chose not to bother finishing him off in favor of looking around for his next opponent, but what he saw instead was legionnaires backing away from their attackers.

Then he heard the words that simultaneously froze a commander's heart and boiled his blood.

"Flee for your lives!"

"It's hopeless!"

"Get back here, you cowards!" Sisenna's voice cut through the noise, but it was too late. More and more legionnaires turned away from the fight and set off running for the woods, dropping their weapons and shields as they fled.

Such a rout was unheard of in the republic's highly disciplined legions. Even in their first war against Esbera, when they were still little more than a city-state and that desert nation was at the height of its power, had their soldiers ever turned and fled from the enemy.

Red-faced and carrying only his sword, the tribune started grabbing legionnaires and shoving them toward the enemy. Some of them were still holding their ground, but all within reach felt the sting of their commander's wounded pride.

A flash of movement to his left seized Raldus' attention before he could intervene, and he raised his shield just in time to block an overhead sword strike. He thrust up with the shield to unbalance his attacker, then swung his own sword around and struck his opponent in the side with enough force to drive him to the ground. A quick stab to the neck ended the threat, then the champion was pushing through his own men toward Sisenna.

He caught up to the tribune who held a legionnaire by the throat with one hand while the other was raised in the air and poised to strike. Ducking beneath the raised arm, Raldus drove his shoulder into the man and forced him away from the whimpering new blood.

"Pull back to the fort!" he shouted in the man's face.

"NO!" Sisenna objected as he twisted away, but Raldus stepped back into his path.

"Regroup at the wall!" he demanded, then shoved him in the direction of the fort.

The tribune swung around as if to strike Raldus, but then a legionnaire stumbled into them. Raldus braced his shoulder against the man to keep from falling, then shoved in the direction of the river when he was once again steady on his feet.

This interruption broke through Sisenna's rage, distracting him long to recover his senses and finally give Raldus a firm nod before turning to the legionnaires and shouting for them to fall back.

"Hold the line!" Raldus commanded those brave souls rallying around him.

"For the people!"

Led by their champion, these men plowed into the dozens of invaders racing after the legionnaires headed for the bridge, knocking many to the ground and forcing the rest to turn and fight or be stabbed in the back.

This rearguard then formed a line and locked shields as they backpedaled toward safety, deflecting one blow after another with both shields and swords. Any invaders attempting to get around them soon found themselves in the dirt or recoiling after getting struck in the face.

"Get across!" Raldus commanded when they finally reached the bridge. He swung his arms wide, forcing the invaders back with the shield in one hand and sword in the other while all but two of the men with him turned and bolted across the stone path arching over the swiftly flowing river.

"We stand with you, Champion!"

The three of them backed onto the bridge far enough for the relatively narrow space to force their attackers to come at each of them one or two at a time, buying their comrades a few more precious seconds of time.

"Now!" Raldus shouted as he thrust forward with his shield to push back his current opponents, then he turned and ran for safety. He saw one of his companions running alongside him from the corner of his eye and the dozens of footfalls chasing them over the crest told him that only enemies remained behind them.

The moment they crested the arch, Raldus raised his sword and swung it down again, signaling the engineers on the other side to cut the ropes holding up the weakened bridge. Stones fell into the river behind them with great splashes, followed by screaming invaders, but Raldus and his companion reached solid ground and turned to confront any opposing soldiers who also made it across.

Only five of them managed it, all of whom charged straight in with swords held high before Raldus could demand their surrender. The bridge guards, fresh from not yet having fought, joined Raldus and his companion in the fight, quickly overwhelming them with greater numbers.

"Surround them!"

The soldiers moved as one to encircle the isolated invaders to prevent their escape into the water, pushing them back with shields and sword points when they threw themselves against the formation.

Darting past the shield wall, Raldus dropped his sword to grab the wrist of the first enemy to challenge him and followed through with a headbutt to the guy's face, bloodying the man's nose with his helmet. When his opponent's sword fell from a loosened grip, Raldus shoved him back into the others still desperately swinging at the shields closing in around them.

The legionnaires followed Raldus' lead and pounced on the half-dozen invaders who still drew breath and relieved them of their weapons. When they continued to struggle, the soldiers used whatever was available to bind the hands of their prisoners behind their backs, even if that meant dropping their sheaths in the grass to use their own belts.

"Take them away," Raldus ordered once they were finally secure.

His men made for the fort, either pushing their prisoners ahead of them or partnering up to drag them in between them when they continued to resist. He retrieved his sword from the grass, then glanced across the river to confirm that the bridge's collapse was successful in forcing the invaders to pause.

Those blue-armored soldiers not bent over with hands on knees or sitting on the grass glared back at him, but none moved to attack.

Satisfied, the champion took a deep breath, then turned and followed after the others. He still held his sword with the point toward the ground, choosing not to sheathe it until after wiping it clean of the crimson staining its bright steel.

"What will it take to stop these people?" Legate Tullus questioned.

From his perch atop the fort's southern gate, he watched the invaders on the opposite riverbank lashing together log rafts. He could also see the remnants of Wolf Legion, including many with the courage to return after fleeing during yesterday's rout, regrouping in the open space between the river and fort wall. It made for some small comfort that the stubbornness of his own people was proving equal to that of their attackers, at least for now.

"There is no stopping a doom sent by the gods," Tribune Lucius remarked as if the invaders' origins was a proven fact.

"They do seem to be ignoring our prayers," Tullus mused.

Although personally unconvinced, he still wondered if some god or gods were behind all of this, such as one previously unknown to them who had grown angry at their lack of worship. The one thing of which he felt sure was that their own gods would not do this to them, but that led to the mystery of why they did not act to save the Naeran people from this curse. Was Keslu waiting for them to prove their worth before intervening or allowing any in his court to do so?

"What are your orders?" Lucius asked once the battered remnants of the legion were in place.

"We fight until there is no other option. That has not changed."

The invaders finished their preparations and began their float across the river, most of them clinging to their rafts like frightened cats while a few stood as straight and tall as possible.

"Let them have it," the legate ordered. The trumpeter beside him sent up a single blast from his instrument, signaling the catapults to unleash their payloads.

Boulders soared over the walls and arced down to the river to strike the rushing water with thunderous crashes. Waves rippled out from the impacts and capsized the nearest craft while great plumes of the muddied liquid crashed down on others to sweep their occupants into the turbulent foam now surrounding them. Hands breached the surface and flailed about for any hold as the soldiers fought against the weight of their armor, but soon disappeared again as they were all swept downstream.

Ropes snapped and wood groaned as the artillery launched a second volley, but while they were yet in the air, four figures in full body armor and wearing white-plumed helmets rushed up on the opposite bank with staffs raised high. The air split with sustained crackling as beams of red shot out and blasted apart many of the rounded stones, the remains of which showered down upon the defenders with light pings as debris bounced off their helmets and armor.

Some stones made it through this defense, but only enough to marginally slow those still making their way across the river, almost all of whom were now lying down and clinging to the damp wood as those still standing furiously paddled in an attempt to reach solid ground as quickly as possible.

Invaders scrambled off the rafts as the first of them reached the embankment, then drew their swords and charged forward with a ferocious shout, breaking the eerie silence with which they'd approached the fighting thus far.

"Archers!" Lucius shouted without awaiting the legate's order, and the archers lining the wall let loose again and again without additional command. The tribune had placed his best marksmen on this wall with the admonition they actually take their time and aim instead of shooting quickly, taking advantage of the one weak spot in the enemy armor of which they were sure. Many arrows indeed pierced masked faces, but the number of those who fell did little to reduce the dark blue tide now sweeping toward the fort.

"Whether it be in fact or legend alone, we will endure," Tullus declared as the two armies below them clashed with the ringing of metal on metal.

"You! Stop them!" Raldus called out to the nearest cavalry officer. He directed the man's attention to the east by pointing his sword at a weak spot in their line where several invaders were crossing and making their way to the side of the fort in an attempt to encircle it.

"Hyah!" the prime shouted as he spurred his horse forward. As he galloped toward his target, he shouted at any nearby horsemen scattered about the battlefield to follow him.

A blade swung at Raldus' head narrowly missed when he ducked beneath the strike. He drove his shoulder into his attacker's chest and forced the man to the ground with him on top. Using his left hand to pin his opponent's weapon hand to the ground by the wrist, Raldus head-butted him in the face, and the impact of helmet on flesh stunned the soldier long enough for the champion to thrust his sword into the man's waist at an upward angle.

After that, he rolled to the right, jumped to his feet, then grabbed another invader by the shoulder from behind and yanked him away from a legionnaire with enough force to send him to the ground. The man's eyes went wide as Raldus raised a foot above him with which he stomped on the man's windpipe before stepping back as the man clutched his throat while sputtering and rolling around.

The waning light was making it hard to see anything, most especially the invaders in their dark armor. Sisenna's death earlier that evening had nearly caused the legion to rout, but Raldus and the other officers managed to pull them together, helped by the fact that they couldn't really go anywhere since they were trapped between the attackers and the fort.

When enough of the enemy had fallen, Raldus prompted the legionnaires to toss aside their own weapons in favor of those dropped by the invaders which helped to even the odds. Dozens of invaders reached the wall at one point and attempted to climb over, but they were all shot dead by the skilled archers or thrown off if they managed to get to the top, becoming an excellent source of weapons for the beleaguered defenders.

Always in the thick of fighting and unwilling to sheathe his dirty sword or toss it aside for fear of losing the weapon gifted to him, Raldus did not yet have one of those swords, but his superior skills meant it was probably best to leave them for those who needed any advantage they could get.

"Champion!" someone shouted. He looked in the direction indicated by the pointed sword to see the invaders at the river finishing up their makeshift bridge of lashed-together rafts. Only the fort's catapults had kept them from getting it in place before now, but they had run out of stones long ago.

A long, sharp trumpet blast from the southern gate sounded retreat for the Naerans, and immediately afterward a volley of arrows either felled the nearest invaders or sent them ducking for cover beneath discarded shields or even the bodies of the slain. If they had ever believed themselves invulnerable, apparently the Naerans had managed to teach them otherwise. Perhaps now the leaders of the army would be able to convince their own people of the same and give them hope where before there was none.

"Rally to the east! Push through!" Raldus ordered as he swept his sword arm over his men as if pushing them forward by his will alone.

All that remained of the legion called up the last of their strength with a mighty shout and surged in the indicated direction. Invaders gave chase, unhindered by archers on the now empty wall, but then a dozen horsemen swept around the legion's right flank to scatter the pursuers by riding straight into them.

Once the footsoldiers were far enough ahead, the cavalry swung back around, spurred their horses into a gallop, and joined the army in exiting the field of battle.

A low horn sounded from across the river, and Raldus glanced over his shoulder to see the attackers stop short and give up the chase.

Another fight lost, and now the invaders were in position to strike at the heart of the republic.

Chapter Eleven

Voices In The Dark

Fires drove back the encroaching darkness as the soldiers finished setting camp and most settled in to eat their evening rations, their voices muted when required to speak.

The Stoneforge Warriors with Raldus had rejoined the army after the battle, one of whom now approached the champion as he made his way to the center of the camp.

"You should rest."

"There's no time for that."

His thoughts firmly on the next task at hand, Raldus strode past the man only a few years his senior who also continued on his way without another word.

The elaborate tent he previously shared with the now deceased Tribune Sisenna sat at the exact center of the camp, but he walked past it and toward the simpler yet just as large tent directly behind it. When the guard lifted the flap upon recognizing the champion, he ducked through the opening in time to hear a man spit.

"Have you learned anything?" Raldus asked the centurion standing between the two wooden poles at the center.

"No, Champion. They know our language, but only speak to insult us," the officer responded as he wiped spittle from his breastplate.

Nodding his understanding, Raldus stepped forward to peer at the six men kneeling on the bare ground near the back, all of whom were naked save for a simple loincloth.

All stared back at him through swollen eyes, the torchlight dancing over them alternating between exaggerating and hiding their bruised and bloody forms. Their hatred for him shone through the lazily drifting smoke and pain-wracked visages, but he felt no pity for them.

"Who are you? Why have you attacked us?"

"You will burn, Savage!"

"Tell me who you are!"

"Your doom."

"What do you want from us?"

"Death."

"Yet, you call me a savage?"

Silence answered this attempt at turnabout.

"Leave them to us, Champion. We'll get them to talk, one way or another," the centurion chimed in, his tone low and menacing.

"There's little else you can do to them without killing them. Perhaps we should leave them to the families of those they've slaughtered. They'll no doubt have thought of some creative ways to express their feelings by now," Raldus threatened.

If the prisoners felt any fear at the prospect of being given over to the festering rage of their victims, it did not show within their hard eyes within battered visages.

Since he clearly wasn't getting anywhere, Raldus met the centurion's gaze and signaled for him to follow with a jerk of his head toward the tent opening.

He breathed deep of the warm evening air as the centurion watched and waited patiently, then looked over at the soldiers sitting and meandering about the camp as he spoke.

"Keep working on them. Do whatever is needed to get them talking, but they are not to be killed, not even one as an example to the others. Understood?"

"Yes, Champion," the centurion confirmed, his armor clattering as he pounded his right fist to his heart in salute. At a nod from Raldus, he ducked back into the tent, leaving his champion to stand there staring into the night.

No answers. Only more questions.

A soft click drew Yalina's gaze to the large wooden door which opened with a slow creak to admit a servant into her chambers in the commander's villa which the triumes had made their home for the duration of their time in the recently captured fort. The eyes of the large-framed woman were fixed on the large bowl in her hands as she stepped over the threshold, but all her care was almost for naught when she looked up and started upon seeing her triume's eyes open and watching her.

"My apologies, Honored One. I did not mean to disturb you," the servant professed, lowering her eyes in respect as she fought to hold the bowl steady from the water set to sloshing from her reaction.

"You did not. I was already awake. Proceed with your duties," Yalina assured her, then sat up in bed. She peeled off the blankets, swung her legs over the side, and slid her feet into the slippers neatly arranged on the floor while the servant proceeded to set the bowl on a tall table before carefully refolding the towel flung over her right arm and placing it beside the bowl.

"Would you like me to stay and assist you?"

"You may leave."

The young woman hesitated as if wondering if this was a test, but then gave a short bow and hurried from the room, carefully closing the door behind her.

Soon refreshed from washing up in the cool, flower-scented water and dressed in her official robes, Yalina exited her chambers to find Avlana awaiting her outside, no doubt summoned by the servant.

"Are you well, my triume?" the leader of her personal guard questioned.

"Nothing is wrong. Send for a scribe. I wish to dictate a letter," Yalina responded, then set off for the stairs leading to a rooftop balcony, her soft shoes whispering across the marble floor. Avlana passed on the command to the door guard, then jogged up to walk at her triume's side in silence, knowing her moods well-enough to understand when she had no desire to explain herself.

The two of them strolled onto the balcony and waited for the scribe who arrived shortly after the sky in the east began to lighten.

"Leave your implements. Avlana will write this letter," the triume commanded. The scribe hastily set his pen and stack of papers on a nearby table, bowed, and hurried back inside as Avlana obediently sat down and picked up the pen.

> *My greetings to you, Vejalon, wise and honorable member of the Holy Triumvirate.*
>
> *By the time this correspondence reaches you, all in the city will have heard of our latest victory over the Naerans with the capture of their fortress at the junction of the two great rivers in this land we seek to gain for future generations. The people will celebrate this, and it is proper they do so, but I fear any reports you have received will not include the true costs of this battle.*

Many of our brave soldiers died in the seizure of this single objective, many more than were predicted could fall to these primitives. The Naerans fought well, with a strength of will which scarcely seems possible. They learned and adapted quickly, and I cannot ignore the possibility they may yet find a way to defeat us in this war by forcing a compromise that fails to meet our needs if not in total.□

My intent with this letter is to ensure you are aware of all the facts to best equip you to guide our people who remain in the city, as I seek to do the same with those who are fighting in this foreign land. Continue to lead with wisdom, courage, and conviction as we have always done and fear will have no room to take root.□

Triume Jasud remains resolved that we will be victorious and hastens to fight the Naerans wherever they can be found. I have called for a period of rest, to which he has agreed, however reluctantly. The will of the triumvirate endures, as does the hope and faith of our soldiers.□

Take heart that this conflict will soon be over, ushering in a new era of prosperity for our people in this land so rich and fertile we need not venture any further.

The sun was fully above the horizon when she concluded what needed to be said, and Yalina indulged herself with the image of it ascending from Zaqulon itself as she gazed at the hazy outline of the distant mountains rising above the wooded plains.

She turned to Avlana as she finished writing the message, then pressed her ring with its diamond symbol into the warm wax before it hardened, and finally commanded that the message immediately be couriered to the city.

As the agent exited the balcony, Yalina saw her tighten her sword belt and place her hand upon the hilt before disappearing into the dim interior.

Despite her careful wording of the letter, the younger woman still understood what was implied, and Yalina allowed herself a small smile of pride at the intelligence of her best agent.

Chapter Twelve

Next Steps

Upon finishing the letter from his trusted colleague in the war zone, Triume Vejalon gently set the sheet of paper on the table next to his chair and peered at the other two black velvet seats. The left corner of his mouth twisted up in a grim smile as he noted yet again how there being no one perched on those cushions made the debate chamber feel so much larger.

As the news from Yalina stewed within him along with her speculations, Vejalon stood and made his way to the chamber's balcony. The sounds of celebration floated up to him the moment he entered the cool night air, revealing that the people had heard about their latest victory. Countless thoughts swirled through his mind as he stood looking down at the crowded streets beyond the wall separating the city proper from the Sacred Heart district where the government offices were situated around the great crystal.

Many of their soldiers died in this recent battle, nearly as many as their studies previously projected would die in the entire war. Some of this was due to the previous failure of their proxy to seize control before their arrival; this much was true, but much of it also came from the Naerans fighting much harder and smarter than anticipated.

How many could they afford to lose before the effort to save their people instead became their undoing?

When the people celebrating below him learned the true cost of the campaign, would they remain committed to the cause?

As difficult as it may be for even a single life to be lost, that wasn't even the worst problem. It was one thing for a person to die, but another thing entirely for his or her soul to be lost while the body continued on, a truth with even deeper implications when applied to an entire people. Was it possible the savagery of this war would yet infect all their hearts and turn their majestic civilization into a monster unleashed upon an unsuspecting world?

Far worse than all those things, if horror could be ranked, was the implied fears a member of the triumvirate had become comfortable choosing his own ego over the will of the other triumes and even the needs of their people. Yalina had not explicitly stated such a concern in her letter, but she no doubt chose not to risk someone else learning of these thoughts and trusted Vejalon to infer her meaning.

From the moment he first met the eldest living triume, Vejalon knew that Jasud harbored a spirit of greed and lust for power held in check only by the traditions of their people. Yalina understod this as well, yet always assured him there was no need to worry about any harm coming of it, but even she was seeing how this war had unleashed the beast from its cage. It was now plain for all those not blinded by his charm that Jasud had spent decades currying favor and placing his loyalists in positions of power.

Could it be possible he now held more sway over the people than both of the other triumes combined?

How would their people be changed by all this death and killing? Would they hold on to their culture of art and science tempered by wisdom, or were they on the path to becoming conquerors and tyrants?

A communal cheer swept through the streets, the voices of tens of thousands merging into one as they rose up to the triume on his balcony.

Their path was set, and only time would tell where it ultimately led them.

The first thing Raldus did after leading the battered remnants of Wolf Legion through the gates of the capital was to see to it that the wounded were taken to the hospital; then he made sure the rest were quartered and fed. All this while a deputy trailed along with persistent reminders of the summons to appear before the senate immediately upon arrival.

The only care he took for himself was to wipe down his dented armor with an old rag, but there was nothing he could do about the bloodstains or the tunic turned dark from days of sweat and filth. When he finally slogged into the senate chamber, many of the senators and the consul wrinkled their noses and looked down at him above raised chins, but he paid them no mind and stood tall as he strode to the center of the room where his father and the legate already stood. In the shadows to his left stood Keid whose gaze Raldus met from the corner of his eyes but did not otherwise acknowledge the grey-robed monk.

"You're late," the senate speaker in sky-blue toga with a green sash accused, standing tall next to the seated consul on the center dais.

"We arrived only a short while ago, and my first task was to find care for the wounded and lodging for the rest," Raldus responded.

"This body does not appreciate being made to wait."

A scathing remark was instantly on Raldus' lips, a sarcastic crack about the difficulty of having to spend a few extra minutes sitting around in silk robes, but then his father cleared his throat beside him. This was enough to remind him to take care with his words which he did by swallowing hard to push down the comment along with his pride.

"I will keep this in mind, Senator."

A low growl accompanied his apologetic words, earning him a side-glance from Mettius, but that was all the politeness he cared to conjure up.

"We were discussing Mettius' discovery that the weapons and armor of the invaders seem to be based on our own designs. Do you have any thoughts on this matter?" the consul changed the subject. The pudgy man shifted his weight on the cushioned seat and adjusted his purple toga before settling his gaze on the man he had named champion nearly one year ago.

This similarity in weapon design was something Raldus also noticed at Fort Nelius, but he didn't see how it was relevant to anything, so he simply replied in the negative.

"What of the prisoners? Have you learned anything from them?"

"No. They see us as little more than animals, much the same as we view the Mortun tribes of the southern swamps, and refuse to speak except to hurl insults."

"Do they not feel pain?"

"They do, but its application has yet to convince them to reveal anything about themselves or their intentions."

The consul leaned back in his cushioned stone chair, his expression growing sour as he looked down at the leaders of his army.

"You have yet to win a single battle against this enemy, unless you count the twelve saboteurs killed at the expense of eighteen of our soldiers, and can't even draw out information from those few invaders you've managed to capture alive. What do you plan to do now to save this city?" the consul accused as he eyed each of them in turn.

"There's nothing to be done! Our destruction is the will of the gods!" a senator cried out.

"They did it to our ancestors and are doing it to us again!"

"It was the old gods who abandoned our ancestors in Tresca, not those we serve now!"

Although the history of Naera's founding was now more legend than hard truth, it was widely accepted that their ancestors fled the destruction of a previous city before wandering for years as refugees. The hostility of the Esberans eventually forced them to brave the mountains deemed impassable by those desert natives. When they did find a way through, they discovered a fertile land almost entirely unspoiled by mankind.

The people blamed their gods for this suffering and turned away from them during their diaspora. Little thought was given to religious matters as they built their new city and tamed the land, but then the first war against Esbera ended in a magnificent victory. Out of gratitude for the perceived favor, the Naerans then adopted the Esberan gods as their own and had worshiped them ever since.

"What does it matter? Our doom is upon us, whatever god or gods sent it!"

Raldus could almost feel Keid forcing himself to remain quiet over there in the corner, but neither of them spoke out against the claim of any other god but the one.

There was a doctrine for the followers of Rosjen that said they must never deny him in front of men, but for all things there was a time and place, and staying silent while others spoke from their beliefs was not the same as denial.

"This time there's nowhere for us to run! Only the ocean awaits us further west!"

How was this hysteria helping anything?

"We should go to the temples and beg the gods for mercy!"

Wondering what they were thinking or if they were going to do anything, Raldus looked at his father and the legate from the corner of his eye, but they were just standing there and waiting.

"We've been doing that! They must want something more. Perhaps we should sacrifice some virgins?"

Now that was something which Raldus would not tolerate, but fortunately the consul chose this moment to restore order.

"That's enough! We are here to discuss the defense of our city, not to guess at the mind of the gods. That is a matter for the priests, not the political leaders of this republic."

None of the senators had a response for him. Many of them glanced nervously at each other while a few glared angrily at the military leaders before them and the rest whispered among themselves.

"Perhaps we should recess to gather our thoughts while the consul discusses matters with the legate and warriors," a senator proposed, and a murmur of agreement rippled through the gallery.

"So be it," the consul confirmed, and the dozens of senators filed out of the room through the two side doors. When they were gone, the consul stepped down from his dais to stand in front of the three men but made sure to stay upwind of Raldus. Keid also joined them, returning the consul's irritated glance with a warm smile.

"I still think there is some significance to the origin of the invader designs for their equipment. Legate?" the consul began.

Now that the setting was considerably less formal, everyone relaxed a little and stepped away to form a semi-circle in front of their nation's leader instead of a straight line.

"Our current designs grew from those of the past, but bear little resemblance to anything from our past or anything we have seen used by anyone else. As such, I must conclude they copied us, although I suppose a priest might claim we copied them through divine inspiration," Tullus replied.

"Master blacksmiths may well have received such inspiration, but why would gods copy mortals?"

"Why would gods fight mortals with mortals?" Keid interjected.

"The ignorant should not speak," the consul chastised.

"Do the origins of these designs actually matter when we have yet to find a way to defeat them?" Raldus interrupted the brewing argument.

"The truth behind those origins may be the very clue we need to craft a defense," Mettius chided.

"Or it might help the people to not to be afraid of them in knowing that the strength of the invaders comes from our own," Tullus added.

"Both points are true, but the champion is right. We don't know enough to reach a conclusion and nothing is served by endless debate," the consul concluded.

The conversation then turned to sharing all else they had learned, such as how to penetrate the enemy armor and the tactics they used. When the subject of the invader's staff weapons came up, Raldus reminded them of how he defended against the one he previously faced. They all agreed this information was of limited usefulness, especially since the weapons didn't seem to be affected by striking the catapult hurled stones at Fort Nelius.

"We are doomed. How can anyone possibly defeat an army of the gods?" the consul eventually despaired as the light filtering through the ceiling window brightened from the sun's noon ascent.

"By remembering that you are fighting mortals, not gods," Keid advocated.

The consul tensed and stood taller in preparation to chastise the monk again, but Legate Tullus spoke first.

"He has a point. No matter who sent the army, its members still die like any other man."

Mettius nodded his approval of the sentiment as the consul looked at the legate, then him, and then back to Keid with a mixture of confusion and annoyance displayed on his features.

Then he took a deep breath and looked at Raldus with brown eyes full of desperate hope.

"What do you think we should do, Champion?"

"I don't know," Raldus responded, sighing from both fatigue and sorrow as he looked at the floor.

He saw from the corner of his eye when Mettius glanced at him, green eyes widened so slightly that only someone who knew him could possibly notice, but the elder warrior did not voice his thoughts. In front of them, the consul's face fell and his whole body drooped as if he was suddenly carrying a great burden.

"The only thing we can do for now is to delay their advance while we prepare the city for a siege. I propose sending a fresh legion to spread out in the land between the invaders and the city to harass their approach," Tullus suggested. They all looked at the consul who just kept looking at the floor at first, but eventually nodded his approval then dismissed them with a wave of his hand before shuffling toward the back door.

The last thing Raldus did was to glance at his father who was once again looking at him, his eyes now narrowed in thought, but just gave the man a quick nod before turning and exiting via the eastern door.

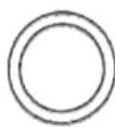

Out of a desire to speak with Raldus, Keid waited in the senate chamber for the others to leave, but grew unsure what to do when the young warrior was the first to depart after the consul's exit. Mettius was next, but the legate remained behind and fixed the monk with an earnest look.

"Would you care to join me for a midday meal?" Tullus asked.

"Certainly," Keid accepted, then fell into step beside the soldier when he started walking.

"Do I understand correctly that the champion has come to believe as you do?"

"That's right."

"I'd like to hear more about that."

"Why?"

"Both of you have a sense of peace and confidence about you that I've never seen before, which is especially interesting given the times," Tullus confessed, eliciting a smile from the monk.

Perhaps his presence here was bearing fruit after all.

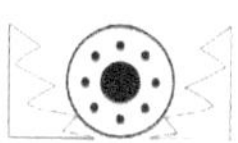

The changes in his son were something Mettius greatly wished to discuss with the boy, but he thought it best to wait, given all that had already happened that day. He could catch up with him once they were both relatively fresh after a night's rest.

It was a sensible plan, but it all changed when he entered the hot water room of the city's smallest bathhouse an hour before dusk. On the far edge of the steamy pool sat Raldus, his head back and eyes closed as his arms kept him propped up on the stone edge. The best time to do something was always the present, and this was as good a place as any for a calm conversation, so the elder Velix made his way over to his son past dozens of other men oddly silent at a normally vibrant time of the day.

He was still many paces away when Raldus' eyes shot open and fixed upon Mettius, the former's warrior instincts alerting him to the approach. Those same instincts quickly identified him to not be a threat, and the young man leaned back again with a sigh as his father lowered himself into the pool heated by a wood-burning furnace beneath its slabbed floor.

"I never thought I would see the day where you didn't have an answer for something or doubted you could win a fight, much less the one where you admitted it," Mettius launched right into the subject at hand.

"Perhaps if you cared more about your own son than the code, you would have seen much more by now," Raldus retorted without looking at him. Neither spoke for several seconds, then Mettius met his son's emerald gaze and responded with words heavy with regret.

"Nobody's perfect, son."

The younger warrior continued staring at him for a bit, then finally sighed as he sat up straight to splash some water on his arms.

"What we face and is being asked of me now is far beyond anything than even I have ever dreamt," Raldus admitted tiredly.

The elder Velix gave a few understanding nods, but hesitated to speak again, then smiled when a thought occurred to him.

"If Proclus were here, he would know what to say," he stated with a sad smile, and Raldus nodded somberly before responding.

"You were always better at enforcing discipline than getting things to make sense," he remarked jokingly, and Mettius couldn't help but smile in acknowledgement of that truth.

"One thing I do know is that every warrior inevitably encounters someone who is better than him, whether it be in technique or raw strength. Only the greats are capable of still finding a path to victory," he related.

"I don't seem to be measuring up at the moment."

"You did it once. Do it again."

This got Raldus to look at his father with his eyes wide and mouth partially agape. Having said his piece, and trusting he'd gotten his point across, Mettius gave him one last quick nod, then dove forward to immerse himself and leave his son in peace with his thoughts.

The morning light filtering through the office's single window was all Raldus needed as he leaned back in the chair behind the desk strategizing methods for stopping the invaders from reaching Naera. Unfortunately, no matter how hard he tried to stay focused, his thoughts kept circling back around to his father's words the previous evening. It wasn't exactly difficult to imagine why given how this stern creature who raised him had never before shown any ability to bend but was now expressing deep thoughts and feelings.

Perhaps the world was ending after all?

He cleared his head with a quick shake, then leaned forward, folded his hands on top of the desk, closed his eyes, and bowed his head.

"Lord Rosjen. You know I'm still getting used to this, and I often wonder if I'm doing it right, but I hope you will listen to me now. Everybody expects me to save them from this evil, but I don't know what to do. Show me the way and grant me peace with what must be done. All truth," he prayed, then turned his chair away from the door and leaned back to stare at the republic map on the wall once more.

He smiled upon remembering the foolishness of having one's back to an open door, but he felt no fear in this place and needed to think without the distraction of people walking past.

As he sat there, the Stoneforge Warrior's Code came to his mind. The words were drilled into him for his entire childhood and he knew them by heart, but despite this familiarity, he now found himself dwelling on them as though they were freshly learned.

Uphold truth and justice and
do not use for personal gain or
boasting.

Acquire resources for the benefit of
family and community, not as an
end in itself.□

The needs of others are of higher
concern than one's own.

A warrior's might exists to fortify

the weak.

Stand firm against the perils of this world.

Life is made purposeful when tempered with the insight of experience.

Fight with purpose and restraint.

Violence is wielded to protect the weak, not to enslave them.□

All lives have value, and it is not one's place to consider himself above another.□

Born among the stones of the valley, trained by the souls within, and sworn to live by the code of my people.

There were many volumes written by the more scholarly warriors interpreting and expanding upon the meaning of that code, or at least there were before the invaders burned Stoneforge, but this and the creed which summarized it was known by heart to all members of the order. As was required of all warriors upon completion of their training, Raldus had sworn to live his life by its teaching after reciting it from memory, but his own interpretation vastly differed from that of all the others.

Up until almost two years ago, that is, when experience taught him what words could not.

Now his fresh perspective revealed something else to him, perhaps the one solitary concept to which all that poetry meant to assign meaning.

He excitedly called out for a messenger to run to the legate and consul requesting a meeting, then rummaged through the pile of parchment on his desk for a map of the city of Naera and another of the whole territory it governed.

His mind said this was not the way to win a war, but his gut insisted it was the right thing to do.

Chapter Thirteen

People Come First

Once again, Raldus stood before the full senate, though this time his armor shone in the sunlight streaming through the windows. To his left stood his father in his leather Stoneforge armor while on his right Legate Tullus wore his segmented armor with gold figurines, his helmet with its fanned blue plume held in the crook of his right arm.

The consul bade Raldus step forward and present his plan to the senate, making no effort to hide the sour look on his face expressing his continued disapproval of the warrior's plan presented to him the previous afternoon. It took Legate Tullus voicing his support for the plan to get the man to even consider calling up the senate to hear it, and even then Raldus had to invoke his status as champion before he agreed.

"Senators of Naera. In speaking for the people, you are no strangers to making hard decisions. The proposal you have come to hear today is likely to be the hardest of all, but I trust you will listen carefully and do what is best for the people," Raldus began, cringing at the formal speech but knowing it was the only way they would ever consider what he was about to say.

He looked around the room, saw that he had everyone's full attention, then took a deep breath before continuing.

"Now that they have secured the south, it is possible the invaders will now proceed through the east and/or west, then across the north to fully encircle our capital city. This is what any other army would do, but it is my belief this one will come straight at us in the presumption they are strong enough to deliver a final blow without any need for such strategies."

This set many of the senators to whispering, and Raldus glanced at the consul who was still angrily glaring at him even while allowing him to speak. After that, he looked at the legate and finally his father, drawing some strength from their steady gazes, and finally back at the gallery as the whispers died down.

"If we stay here, our people will die. Our best chance for victory in this war is to send our citizens away to take refuge wherever it can be found, be it in the northwest mountains, the great forest, or even Kostrai. When that is done, we take all the forces we can muster to Izagion to make a stand behind their legendary walls," he concluded.

The senators instantly shot to their feet, shouting uproariously. Most of their words were unintelligible, but the stronger voices managed to rise above the rest.

"Abandon Naera! Are you mad?"

"Never has a foreign army stepped foot inside these walls!"

"This is unthinkable!"

"Senators! Please!" Tullus pleaded as he stepped forward with left hand palm-forward at shoulder height.

None of the politicians heeded him and continued to hurl objections and even accusations at their champion.

"Traitor!"

"*Never* question my son's loyalty," Mettius barked, his many years of bellowing orders at recruits filling his voice with enough power to pierce the noise and quiet the senators.

It took a few seconds for all of them to fall silent, reconsider any inclination to challenge the elder warrior's authoritative glare, and sit back down; a fact for which Raldus was grateful as it gave him time to recover from that stinging remark on his character.

As the last of the shouts faded to whispers, the consul rose from his seat and redirected his stern gaze to his fellow politicians, speaking before Raldus made a decision on what to say next.

"I do not like the idea of abandoning our city any more than you do, but this man is the Champion of the Republic and you *will* show him respect," he admonished, and a few in the gallery sounded their agreement.

"To run from a fight goes against my very nature, a warrior's nature, but I must place the lives of the people above all else. If we keep using the same tactics we've always used, all of us will die," Raldus spoke up.

"If our destruction is the will of the gods; nothing we do will prevent it!" a senator challenged.

"That's right! If this is to be our end, then let us meet it in the comfort of our own homes!" another shouted.

"The one true god would not do this," Raldus growled, his patience on the matter nearly gone.

The statement instigated scornful laughter among many, some of whom shot to their feet again to shout accusations of blasphemy down at him. Even the consul, once again seated, put his face into the palm of his hand and started lightly stroking his forehead with his fingers.

"All gods respect strength, and it is up to us to prove ourselves worthy of their respect," Mettius interjected after stepping forward to place a hand on Raldus' shoulder.

"We will fight and die for this city, no matter where that fight takes us," Tullus added.

"Like those cowards who ran at Nelius?"

"Many more stood their ground and made the enemy pay for their victory with much blood. Those who did run will suffer the consequences, one way or another," Tullus growled.

"Will the Izagions even let our legionnaires into the city?" a relatively calm voice questioned.

Although officially in Naeran territory, the city of Izagion on the northern border existed as an independent city-state. When their ancestors were conquering the land after building Naera, they were unable to breach that city's ancient walls which led right up to the enormous lake now forming the northern border. With no way inside or to cut off the city's access to fish, the Naerans eventually had to agree for them to continue governing themselves in exchange for the establishment of their own naval fort nearby and free passage across the lake.

Although their relations had been friendly ever since, there was no guarantee the Izagion leaders would agree to stand with the Naerans in battle against the invaders. It was always possible they would decide to leave their former adversary to their fate in the hopes of making a new deal with the invaders.

"We should send a deputy to ask while we continue our deliberations," another senator suggested.

The consul looked around as Raldus watched expectantly. His own interpretation of the overall mood was that they were willing to do this much, even if it was only to placate their champion because they fully expected the Izagions to refuse.

"Very well. We will send an envoy to Izagion to discuss the matter with them," the consul consented.

"In the meantime, we should begin evacuating people from the city, starting with the sick and injured, then the women and children. Even if we do stay to mount a defense, we'll have a better chance of surviving a siege with fewer mouths to feed," Tullus suggested, and Mettius nodded his approval while Raldus simply looked on.

"Do it. The three of you can leave now. We have much to discuss among ourselves," the consul agreed. Each of them gave a short bow, then walked out together.

When soldiers arrived at the hospital where Keid was ministering to the sick and their caretakers, pitching in with the work where he could, he helped start the process of getting them ready to move. As they worked, he learned from them that the army might be withdrawing all the way to the northern border, which would leave the rest of the territory at the mercy of the invaders. It also appeared that they didn't yet know where they would be sending the evacuees, at least not all of them.

Once he was sure the process was running smoothly, he collected Katriel from the city library, then went in search of Raldus.

"Where will we go when the Naerans flee this city?" Katriel asked as they set off down the cobblestone street.

"I will remain with Raldus wherever this fight takes him, ministering to him and the people around him, but I feel it is time for you to return home," Keid revealed.

"Have I done something wrong?"

"Not at all. Thousands of people live here, and all of them must now find shelter elsewhere. I intend to offer our town as one such shelter, and need you to convey word to Abbot Jerald should Raldus believe this is prudent."

"Is it wise to take in so many strangers?" Katriel questioned as he looked around at the people in their colorful tunics or dresses rushing about them.

"Would you abandon them to their fate? Is that what Rosjen asks of us?"

The younger monk gave his elder a wide-eyed glance, then looked to the ground in shame and whispered his reply.

"No."

"We are called to do what we can for all those who are in need. The rest is in the hands of our Lord."

They walked the rest of the way to the city garrison barracks in silence where Keid learned from a soldier standing guard that Raldus was currently working in the main armory. Keid thanked the man, then led the way by following his directions down the smoky main corridor lit only by torches in wall sconces to the heavy wooden door at the opposite end of the building from the entrance.

Although the wood was thick and banded with metal, the door seemed light on its well-oiled hinges as Katriel pulled it open for his elder. The next room was lit by the sun streaming through high, narrow windows, and in the center between shelves of spears and swords, the two monks found their warrior companion. He looked up from the table in front of him at the sound of their entrance, then back down at his work without a word.

They made their way across the dirt floor, and Katriel gasped when he saw the full set of dark blue armor laid out on the table.

"I didn't realize it covered their entire body. How do they move?" the junior monk remarked as he leaned in.

"The metal is thin, and each plate attaches to the next by a hinge of sorts," Raldus explained without looking up. Katriel reached out a hand as if to touch the various pieces of shaped metal or the single piece of thick cloth in the shape of a man beneath it, but pulled back before doing so. Meanwhile, Keid merely gazed upon Raldus, taking note of his furrowed brow and squinting eyes.

"How are the two of you doing? I'm sorry I haven't been able to talk to you much," Raldus eventually continued.

"We are well, learning much about the republic and its people, and have even gained a few converts. You are burdened enough. Do not worry about us," Keid assured him.

Raldus acknowledged his words with a nod but didn't look away from the breastplate laid out on the table before him.

"What is the problem?" Keid asked.

"If we're going to use this armor, we need to change the color so we'll recognize our own people from theirs. However, this paint doesn't buff out to restore the metal's natural shine, so the only thing to do is paint it a different color. Turns out there's more to consider in choosing what color that should be than I would have thought, such as finding something cheap that isn't already assigned to any faction," Raldus explained.

"I hear your army will be retreating to the north soon," Keid went ahead and broached the subject foremost on his mind. The warrior's gaze snapped up to meet the monk's own with eyes narrowed in what could only be interpreted as suspicion.

"It is not *my* army. You need to start thinking of yourselves as being as much a part of the republic as the rest of us if you truly intend to reach people," Raldus asserted.

"But we aren't part of it," Katriel protested, only to look down and away when the warrior fixed him with a stern gaze.

"I meant no offense, and apologize for not properly considering my words," Keid spoke up, then continued after Raldus nodded his forgiveness.

"We came here to ask if we need soldiers guarding the monastery."

The warrior's eyes grew distant as he no doubt thought of his wife and soon to be born child, and when he spoke he did so with thinly masked fatigue.

"No. It's actually one of the safest places right now. The only way it will be in danger is if we fail here, and even then it will likely be some time before the invaders find their way to it. You should return there."

"I will stay here to help and minister where I can, but Katriel will return and prepare a place for those fleeing this conflict. Do you believe that would be acceptable?"

Raldus silently watched them, and Keid patiently waited for his reply. He could only guess at the thoughts running through his young friend's mind right now, everything from his concern for his family to his own experiences with the monk's isolationist policy.

"Such a decision is up to you. As a newcomer, I am in no position to speak for either the monastery or town. No one in the government or army will care about anything beyond available infrastructure, and some might even be grateful, but be sure it's what you want to do before offering because they won't let you take it back," he eventually told them.

"I understand. Rosjen be with you," Keid accepted, then turned and left.

On day six of the army's respite she had arranged with her fellow triume, Yalina strolled through the captured fort, smiling serenely at those who stood to honor her passing.

Their first task following their victory here was to construct a proper cemetery within the fort's walls for their dead. They would have preferred to send the bodies of their slain back home to Zaqulon, but there was no room left for burials within the crater and these brave souls deserved a better memorial than a simple incineration was capable of providing.

Nearly all of the Naerans killed in the battle were outside the walls at the time, so the Zaqulons waited to deal with those bodies until after their own fallen were interred in the ground. When they did dispose of them, the only effort they made was to stack the corpses and burn them.

After that was finished, those on burial detail joined the others already hard at work repairing and improving the fort's defenses as much as they could without first deconstructing them as well as setting up proper living and working spaces in the buildings. A crew of engineers also built a new bridge over the river by using the materials from the old one and fresh resources as needed.

When the majority of the work was completed a week later, Jasud had wanted to continue their advance, but Yalina convinced him to reward the soldiers with a few days of rest. The first two of those days passed in solemn silence, but now song and laughter filled the fort and nearby camp as soldiers and officers alike spoke of their impending final victory.

On this day, Yalina's walk took her to the fort's central forum where she discovered Jasud speaking with Zishna Bujon, the army's top commander and one of the eldest triume's personal agents.

"How long do you intend to idle here?" Jasud accused when she approached.

"Three or four more days," she responded casually.

"We are ready to move now and finish this," Bujon declared.

"Are you sure about that?"

The zishna's only response was a narrowing of his eyes as he pressed his lips together until they formed a thin line. Since he was clearly unwilling to admit his confusion, Yalina chose to answer the question for him.

"This is the first time leaving the city for most of these soldiers, and this campaign is their first experience with actual combat. Such experiences take time to process."

"They can handle it."

"Of that I have no doubt, but hundreds of their comrades died in this last battle. I believe it is for the best that they have some time to mourn those losses and gather courage for the next fight," Yalina insisted.

Not wanting to contradict the word of a triume, Bujon did not respond even as his eyes burned with resentment.

"So be it. We will wait three more days; then we must move on. It will take at least that long to reach Naera, which gives them more than enough time to process their *feelings*," Jasud finally acquiesced, twisting the last word out of obvious disdain.

Yalina bowed her head in agreement, then walked off to return to the commander's villa, having been seen by the people enough for one day.

Chapter Fourteen

Hard Choices

"Politics, psh. The code has never made more sense," Raldus grumbled to his father as they walked through the forum on their way to the southern gate.

"One has nothing to do with the other," Mettius chastised.

I never said it did, Raldus thought as he rolled his eyes, but he said nothing aloud. The sets of armor captured from the invaders had been distributed among the warriors, but there wasn't enough for everyone, so the two of them were equipped with their own Stoneforge leather armor. Both agreed they preferred the others to have the superior protection, and Raldus chose this gear for the greater mobility and stealth it afforded in the field. The armor gifted to him by the monks he'd entrusted to Keid's care for the time being.

At least enough of the enemy swords were available for each of them to have one now swinging in leather sheaths from their left hips.

His current state of annoyance was due to the senate spending the first two days following his proposal arguing over their next course of action, during which those most opposed to his plan even blocked the sending of the agreed-upon envoy to Izagion. They refused to allow Raldus before the full assembly, but the legate with his greater political experience managed to convince several of them to meet with him individually and in that way they finally gained enough support to have a deputy sent to the city on the third day.

This growing friendship with Tullus was a curious one. At first, he thought the man just wanted to get close to him to share in the fame brought to him by his status as champion, but now he believed there was much more to it than that. A belief reinforced by how much time he and Keid were spending together. He was not privy to the nature of their discussions, but knew there was only one subject on which the monk would spend so much time.

Could it be that the republic's top military leader was entertaining the idea of converting?

A battle cry drew the attention of the warriors as they passed the arena dedicated to the god of heroes, a place where both father and son had spent considerable time in better days. Spectacles for the masses were often held there, but it was most often used as a training ground for fighters of all disciplines and backgrounds. It was also one of the few places Stoneforge Warriors trained with men outside of their order, and on rare occasions they even displayed their skills in games set against other fighters, animals, or even between their own members. It was not the goal in these competitions to kill, but the inherent danger meant contestants did die from time to time.

Father and son returned their attention to the street and continued on their way encouraged by the fact someone was using this delay to sharpen their skills.

Another unexpected benefit to the senate's deferred action was the arrival of three Stoneforge Warriors from the north on the first day, then five more from Esbera on the second. This brought their numbers up to sixteen when including Primus who was still scouting around Stoneforge for the invader's origin point.

"You should be the one to stay here and put your own plan into action," Mettius complained as they neared the city's southern gate.

"The invaders have paused for now, but when they start moving again, it won't take them long to reach the city. We need to do something to slow them down," Raldus insisted.

"I'm not debating that. What I'm saying is that you should stay here and I lead the men in the field," Mettius argued.

"I'm wasted on politics. You and the legate will get much farther with the senators than I ever will," Raldus asserted.

Any further arguments remained unspoken as they reached the gate plaza where the other warriors were already assembled, all but one of them clad in the freshly painted enemy armor which was now theirs. The one for whom they did not have an armor set wore only his tunic with a sword belt around his waist and a pair of cheap sandals, claiming he would get his own armor soon enough.

Raldus had chosen a soft green color to replace the midnight blue, mostly for how easily it contrasted with the blue, but also because it would help the wearers stay hidden in the woodlands and grass. The warriors did not wear cloth masks like the enemy soldiers, leaving their faces open beneath the helmets and between the ear flaps, granting them an extra layer of distinction despite it being done for comfort rather than practicality.

"Where are the consularians?" Raldus asked, referring to the consul's personal guard, all but one unit of which had been placed at his disposal for this mission.

"Already in the field," Brutus answered.

"They're probably trying to get a head start so they look better when they return," Mettius grumbled, eliciting chuckles from a few of the warriors despite his lack of a smile indicating he didn't mean it as a joke.

"Then it's time we also get on the move," Raldus remarked as he stepped up to the others, but stopped and looked back when Mettius spoke again.

"I have something to say before you go. All of you here were my students at one time or another, and you should know that I am proud of each and every one of you, none more so than my son whose wisdom has grown to match his strength. Fight well, remember the code, and you will no doubt return with reason to make me yet more proud."

Raldus stared at his father, wondering what he could possibly say to such an outburst of the like he'd never heard before, but the veteran warrior simply put his right hand to left breast with index finger over the middle and the other two folded into his palm in the Stoneforge salute, then spun around and walked away without another word.

"Well, we're definitely going to die," one of the warriors remarked, causing the others to laugh. Even Raldus smiled at the joke made at his stern father's expense as he walked through the group and led them out the gate.

The muted sounds of a sudden commotion on an otherwise normal, quiet day broke into the abbot's thoughts. He set the quill beside the half-filled parchment as he grumbled 'what now', then stood up, wincing as his aged joints cracked and popped, and made his way over to the blue and red stained-glass window dominating the wall behind his desk.

Upon looking down into the plaza below the monastery, he spotted a mass of grey slowly traversing the stone courtyard toward the steps to the main building. Jerald rubbed the weariness from his eyes with a thumb and finger, then focused on the group to see that it was several monks surrounding a single one, badgering him with questions with no regard for the weariness apparent in each step the man took.

Times like this caused Jerald to wonder if it would be wise to invent a vow of silence for their order to stop the monks from behaving like such fools.

When the group reached the bottom of the steps, the source of their attention looked up at the abbot's window and he finally recognized him as Katriel, the young monk who had accompanied Keid and Raldus on their mission. He paused there at the steps, staring up as his body practically vibrated from tension, then took a deep breath and looked ahead as he finally started up the stairs.

The man was clearly on his way to speak with him, so Jerald returned to his chair behind the large wooden desk and made himself comfortable as he waited.

"Enter," he commanded when the single knock came a few minutes later.

The thick wooden door silently swung open and to the abbot's considerable relief, Katriel entered the room alone. His visitor shut the door again before shuffling over to the desk where he stood with head bowed to await his elder to speak first.

"Are Keid and Raldus well? Why are they not with you?" Jerald asked as the most important item to be established.

"Yes, Abbot. They have not been harmed, and remain committed to their tasks. I was sent back to inform you of current circumstances," Katriel started, but then hesitated mid-sentence to take a shaking breath before finishing. "And to make a request."

The abbot's eyes narrowed as he considered what the troublemaking Keid could be after this time while the junior monk continued to avoid his gaze by staring at the floor.

"Tell me," Jerald directed. His voice was little more than a whisper, but was easily discerned in the quiet room.

Katriel's dark eyes darted about the candlelit room, then he steadied himself with another deep breath and delivered the entirety of the message at last.

"The invaders are prepared to attack Naera itself, and the people are fleeing the city before that happens. Keid wishes to shelter some of them here and sent me to prepare for their arrival."

Complete silence fell on the room. A silence so thick that the shuffling of the younger monk's robes as he shifted his weight from one foot to the other scarcely seemed to penetrate. It also appeared to grow darker in the already dim space, and even the candles ceased their flickering to cast steady shadows upon the walls and freeze the space in this moment.

"No."

The abbot's voice was so low that even he had to wonder if he'd actually said it, but then Katriel stood up straighter and lifted his face toward the abbot, although he still did not meet his gaze by staring at the wall behind the old man instead.

"Is it not our responsibility to help those in need?"

"Not at the cost of our own people."

"Won't Rosjen protect us?"

This sudden act of defiance from his junior sent Jerald launching from his chair to stand with his hands on the desk, all his aches and pains forgotten as he glared at the boy before him.

Curse that Keid and his naïve idealism! How many others would he insist on infecting with his dangerous ideas of opening their doors to all people?

"Watch your tone."

"I don't mean any disrespect, Abbot, but why can't we help them?" Katriel insisted.

This set the abbot to pacing behind his desk as he fought to contain the fury boiling up within him.

"The only way we stay safe here is by knowing who we can trust! Raldus may have earned that trust, for now, but his culture is one of violence and greed. There can be no trusting so many of them all at once. They can go hide somewhere else!" he raged.

"No, they can't."

The youngster's quietly confident tone came as a splash of cold water on the abbot who ceased his pacing and looked into the soft brown eyes of the other monk which finally met his own.

Looking at him now, Jerald found himself wondering where this meek, inexperienced boy had suddenly found so much courage to stand up to him where before he would have fled the room at the first rumblings of anger from the leader of his order. Could this be Rosjen's spirit at work, compelling the young man to open Jerald's eyes to the truth?

"Explain," he demanded, his tone betraying no emotion.

"The invaders already control the republic's southern lands. Those who fled the conquered areas sought safety in the capital, but now that is also in danger. They need a safe place to go."

A sudden weariness took hold of the abbot, and he stumbled back to his chair and sank into it, propping himself up with arms on his desk but continuing to hold his head high for the benefit of his subordinate.

"If what you say is true, then not even this place will remain safe for long."

"It is my understanding that Raldus has a plan and only needs time to implement it. Most of the people will be sheltering in other towns and cities, but we can take in some of them, caring for the sick and wounded if nothing else."

One last look into Katriel's eyes revealed the fear and suffering he'd seen these last few weeks and the unshakeable conviction to do something about it that had come as a result. As he reflected on this, Jerald felt his own fears and doubts suddenly become small and insignificant compared to all that was happening.

Was it enough to survive even as the world burned down around them?

"Rest tonight, then go with the supply runner and two hunters to meet these people and lead them here. We will prepare a place for them," he finally relented.

Katriel acknowledged the directive with a short bow, then hustled from the room.

Once the door was secure and he was alone, Jerald pushed himself up and ambled around the desk into the center of the room where he carefully lowered himself into a kneeling position.

If they were going to do this, he needed to pray and ask for his heart to be in the right place as he cared for these strangers while continuing to look after the needs of his own people.

Chapter Fifteen
Sanctuary

"Deputy Servius of the Naeran Republic Senate here to serve as ambassador to the Izagion city council."

The deputy announced himself and his intent upon reaching the Izagion gate, leaning forward in his carriage to give the linen-armored guard a clear view of the blue stripe running the length of his tunic.

"We're all impressed. Let's see your mark of authority," the guard drawled. Servius glowered at him, then snapped his fingers at the prime in command of his guard detail. The man wearing a green-plumed helmet and shining steel breastplate nudged his mare forward and handed down an unbound scroll to the guard.

The guard unrolled the parchment, skimmed the legal writing, then verified the wax seal of the consul at the bottom.

"Go on through," he grunted upon handing back the scroll.

Although tempted to give this cur a lesson in proper respect, Servius chose to say nothing else and simply raised his chin as he passed through the gate. Such formalities would not be necessary if his ancestors had successfully conquered the city, but as it was, the treaty recognizing the republic's claim to the surrounding territory also marked the city as an independent entity with its own guardsmen operating inside its walls.

Those walls which now rose behind Servius and his retinue had long been a mystery to all who beheld them, having stood before the arrival of the current inhabitants and whose strength had withstood the Naeran siege during the latter part of the city's expansion of its influence in the region.

As they turned a corner on the dirt street, the deputy peered around the blue curtains lining the inside of his carriage at the unnaturally dark stone stretching to either side of the gate, marveling at its seamless facade before the lower half disappeared behind the wooden buildings.

The true means of its construction had long eluded even the best of Naera's engineers, even after their attempt to replicate it when constructing the bridge over the massive lake separating this land from the northern regions. Most assumed they were built by gods who either changed their minds about living there or were driven off by jealous rivals who then abandoned the site.

Perhaps the invaders were sent by those same gods to reclaim what they believed to be rightfully theirs?

The buildings making up the city itself were rather crude in comparison. Most were constructed from wood logged in the nearby forests, the tallest of which still fell short of the height of the walls by at least a quarter.

As the deputy's party made its way through the city, these stores, warehouses, and homes gave way to more impressive structures of grey stone hewn from the quarry at Stoneforge and hauled at great expense across the entire breadth of the republic to form the government buildings and more elaborate houses.

Finally, at the center of it sat the only other structure left by the unknown builders, an elaborate palace in which now resided the Izagion city council. The carriage pulled up in front of this massive building of dark stone, the same as that which composed the walls but was not to be found anywhere else in Naera or the surrounding lands, and Servius gazed upon it as his guards dismounted around him. No matter how many times he saw this structure, it never failed to impress with its scope and architecture.

Where any other building of this type was composed of multiple wings or connecting structures, this one was a single unit the size of a small arena. It rose multiple stories above the surrounding stone courtyard, each level smaller than the one below and centered within it. The top level was exactly one-eighth the size of the bottom and featured a smooth, flat top in the center of which was a large, empty slot that left little clue as to what was originally meant to go inside. Shortly after their arrival in the city, the Izagion leadership filled in this slot with dirt to create a small park with grass and a single tree, frustrating the studies of the Naeran engineers who came later.

The deputy's six guards formed lines on either side of his carriage door, then the prime stepped up and opened it. Servius nodded his thanks to the legionnaire as he pressed his tunic to his stomach and descended the two steps to the stones below. Once he reached the center of the square formation, the guards turned in place and walked in sync with him to the palace entrance, a wide set of unadorned stone doors already standing open to admit them.

They entered at a nod from the guardsmen in black leather without so much as slowing their pace. Braziers lit their way down the cavernous main hall, their footsteps echoing despite the massive tapestries hanging on the walls depicting major events in the city's history. Halfway down this hall, a single corridor in either direction linked this space to rooms around the exterior while this one continued straight to the center where the council of five men administered the city from within a great chamber extending into the floor above.

"Thank you for meeting with me," Servius announced after leaving his soldiers at the chamber's entrance and marching into the center of the room.

"We are always happy to meet with an official from the Naeran Senate," the skinny, pale man at the center of the dais, the city's potentate, responded cordially.

Although their long relationship of open travel and trade led many Izagions to adopt the Naeran clothing style of tunics and sandals, these men still wore shirts, pants, and shoes like those of their ancestors as a symbol of their independence. The only difference was that they were now made from imported silk, or linen for the lower classes who also preferred the tradition, instead of wool as in the past.

"I wish it were under better circumstances. As I am certain you are already aware, a powerful army has invaded our lands and now threatens the city of Naera itself."

"Yes, it seems that the republic is beset by many troubles these days," the potentate insinuated, any potential meaning hidden by a placid expression.

"Clearly, this time the great Naeran army is incapable of fighting back," another official remarked.

"That's enough!" the potentate declared before Servius could respond, then continued in the same calm tone as before, "There is no reason to insult our guest."

"It is true this enemy is strong, but we *are* fighting back. In fact, our champion has developed an impressive new strategy which he is confident will turn this war in our favor," Servius boasted.

"I presume that is why you are here. What have you come to ask of us?"

"The plan is to evacuate the citizens of Naera to any remaining safe haven and bring the bulk of our forces here to your city. This is the most defensible position in the land, and we need that advantage to counter the powers wielded by these invaders."

This revelation set the officials to whispering. Servius could not hear the words, but a seething anger was clear in their tones.

The potentate quietly listened to the others, then held up his right hand to silence them.

"Our two peoples have long enjoyed a prosperous trading alliance, but this does not change the fact that Naera laid siege to our city upon first discovering it, and has limited our ability to do anything outside our walls ever since. Why would we endanger ourselves on your behalf now?"

"For all we know, this is a ploy for you to garrison the city and finish what your ancestors started!" the same official from before blurted out.

"I assure you that we have no interest in seizing control of your city. If we harbored ambitions to expand our territory and power, we would have conquered Kostrai long ago, not to mention the rest of Esbera. Neither possesses the ability to stop us like you do, yet we continue in peaceful trade with one and do not overextend ourselves with the other. This is about saving our people, nothing else."

"*Your* people!" the official spat.

"And yours. Do you really believe these invaders will stop once they destroy us? They will come for you when they are ready."

"We will resist them, as we did you. Our walls will protect us," the potentate insisted, and the deputy couldn't help but let out a frustrated sigh.

"These invaders have weapons far beyond anything seen before. Many believe them to have been sent by the gods themselves, and it has been suggested they are also the ones who built this palace and the city walls before you claimed them as your own. Even if these things are not true, when they come for you, they will do so with unimaginable fury. Would it not be better to meet this threat with our battle-hardened legions at your side rather than alone with your tiny garrison of untested guards?"

The potentate glanced at the other officials, all of whom had their heads down, some staring at the floor while others rested his chin in his hands.

"We need time to think about this," the potentate declared.

"There is no time. The invaders are within days of our city, and we need every moment of that time to evacuate our people and establish a proper defense elsewhere. If that is not to be here, then let me know now so we can make other plans."

"You already said there is nowhere else for you to go," the belligerent official accused.

"That is not true. I said this city is the most defensible option, not the only one. Fort Tryit is also a possibility with the mountains on either side preventing encirclement and the road to Esbera providing a route of escape. There is also the fort constructed by the rebel Tallio Atroni near Pralacus Templum which can be adapted to serve our needs, but neither of these places afford us the chance, or hope, of victory as does Izagion."

Satisfied with this explanation, the potentate glanced once more at the other officials who each met his gaze and returned an affirming nod, albeit reluctantly.

The old ruler sighed, then peered down at his guest and announced that they would fight with the Naeran people.

Nothing else needed to be said, so Servius spun around and exited the chamber.

"Prime, hasten back to the city and report the Izagion decision to the senate. I will remain here and make preparations," he commanded the officer in charge of his guard detail as they traversed the imposing entrance hall.

"Half of my men will stay here with you," the prime insisted.

"No. Take them all."

"I must protest, Deputy. Your safety..."

"The safety of the message you carry is far more crucial, and I am in no danger within these walls. Go! Now!"

The prime hesitated, his mouth open as if to argue further, but then he closed it and nodded to the deputy before jogging off with the other soldiers on his heels. Though they were no doubt as tired as he was after their journey, Servius knew they would not even spend the night, departing immediately with the knowledge that the best chance for their people lay in mobilizing as soon as possible.

As he watched them go, the deputy felt not only pride in this display of devotion from the republic's legionnaires, proving the confidence of their people, but also a sense of relief that his own tour of service was long behind him during a more peaceful era.

There was little else he could do now but hope that the champion was right about abandoning their city for a more fortified position and that they weren't handing their capital over to the invaders only to die later anyway.

The morning cleanup done, Ariela set her rag to dry on the rim of the wooden bucket beside the kitchen table, then placed both hands in the small of her back and leaned into them as she stretched. Most of the pain in her back released with a satisfying pop after which she sighed, set both hands atop her rounded belly, then looked out the window at the grey sky slowly turning to blue from the first rays of dawn.

Raldus was out there somewhere, fighting against incredible odds to preserve the peace of this place and others like it. His calling was to stand against evil and face whatever dangers it brought, even if that meant being far from home when his firstborn arrived in the world.

A second long sigh made manifest the sorrow she felt at being so far from him, too far to look after him when he no doubt refused to rest or treat his wounds. There was nothing she could do as his wife but pray for Rosjen to look after her husband and surround him with people who would protect him, even from himself.

She smiled upon remembering that Keid had gone with him. If anyone could deal with Raldus' ego, it was that equally stubborn monk.

The crowing of a rooster broke into her thoughts, snapping her back to reality, and she made her way into the front room where a basket filled with bandages, a jar of cheap wine, and clean cloths awaited by the door. Those fleeing the cities that Abbot Jerald had agreed to shelter would be arriving today, and her experience with Raldus last year made her invaluable when it came to providing the sick and injured with the best of care.

She may not be able to be there for her husband, but there was nothing stopping her from being a helper and comforter to others in need.

The first to arrive through the stone arch serving as the sole entrance to the walled community of Our Sacred Refuge was a team of five soldiers, their spears lowered to clear the ceiling and eyes narrowed as they settled upon the abbot and the dozen monks assembled behind him. Jerald gave the officer a short nod who returned the gesture before raising a hand to signal his men to hold their spears upright.

As they approached, Jerald noticed the leather and metal comprising their armor was not shining in the early afternoon sun as he'd expected, calling into question the reputed rigidity of the army's discipline. Then he berated himself for the snap judgement, reminding himself that these people had been traveling for days and that he did not have the knowledge or experience to determine by sight alone if the equipment was well-maintained despite the state of its cleanliness.

"Welcome to Our Sacred Refuge. We offer you the peace and safety of our home, and ask only that you honor it with the same care and respect," the abbot greeted the man with a green plume on his helmet in a fan.

"We are grateful for your hospitality. I assure you that my men will behave themselves and will see to it our citizens do the same," the officer responded, his rough voice tired but strong.

The abbot acknowledged this with a short nod and the officer nodded to the man at his right who turned and jogged back to the arch. Meanwhile, the monks stepped around their abbot to line up by the arch and receive their guests, after which the remaining soldiers took up position at the end of the lines, stretching between them to create a box. Jerald waited until all was ready, then took a single step back and to the side and looked at the women waiting at the far edge of the plaza and gave them a single nod. Ready to serve, they proceeded forward with all the speed their burdens and grace of their sex would allow.

He was not surprised to see young Ariela among them, heavy with child but steady in purpose. Beside her strode the middle-aged Naomi carrying one basket precariously balanced atop another, no doubt having insisted on bearing the load of her younger companion.

Hushed voices brought his attention back to the arch where the first of the refugees were now coming through. The soldiers now stood in the square, their spears now leaning against the wall to free their hands for wax tablets to which they referred as each citizen stepped up, then made a mark before directing them to a monk who proceeded to lead them into the plaza where the women waited before heading back for another charge.

The first to come through bore others on stretchers, some of whom were soldiers judging by their physiques, but many were common folk that were a mix of men, women, and even children. One of these, a little boy, passed by Jerald as he stood there supervising, allowing him to see that both hands were heavily bandaged as was his face with a single opening for his nostrils, above which remained only a few clumps of scraggly hair amid blackened skin.

After these came those who could still stand and walk under their own power, some of whom also bore signs of varied injuries, but all of which were clad in little more than rags that could scarcely be recognized as the tunics or dresses they used to be.

This was exactly the fate from which he'd always striven to protect his own people, but now he saw that in his stubbornness, he'd failed to realize that they were not the only ones in need of such care. Had he been keeping their bodies safe this whole time at the cost of their souls?

Monk Elizar came near on his way back from delivering a family to the small park at the west side of the plaza where they could await permanent placement, and the abbot stopped him with a gentle hand on his arm.

"Stay wary and let me know if anything transpires."

Though his expression conveyed confusion, Elizar nodded his obedience, then Jerald walked away toward the monastery's main building where the rest of the monks remained at their regular duties. Hands which were put to better use at other tasks, such as in gathering fresh clothes and food for these people.

He may be a stubborn old man, but even he had the power to change when the need became clear.

In the dark of night made deeper by the cloud-veiled sky, Raldus crept up to the rear of the invader camp. A shadowy outline rose above the tall greenish grass, the unnatural shape far closer to him than the light and sounds up ahead suggested the edge of the camp should be, and he knelt down below the gently swaying stalks to listen for any signs of danger.

He glanced back at his fellow warriors to see only vague shapes in the night, almost missing them in their invader armor. The green paint he'd chosen had darkened from the midnight-blue beneath it which worked even better than expected to blend its wearers into their surroundings.

Although their raids had netted them more sets of armor from their enemy, the champion was still clad in his brown leather Stoneforge armor. They weren't equipped to paint those things in the field, and he didn't want to end up killed by one of his own men, so for now they were hiding them wherever prudent until they could be taken or sent back to an armorer. He still would have preferred the armor given to him by the monks for the reminder of God and home, but they were all better off without its shiny steel when stealth was required.

When he focused back on the camp and snuck forward a few more paces, he spotted three soldiers beside a single canvas tent most likely meant to serve as a sentry post. They were learning from past raids to actually make an effort to protect themselves, but still had a long way to go. Such a pitiful showing wouldn't stop an ambush conducted by regular soldiers, and was merely insulting to the warriors of Stoneforge.

The champion held up his left hand and waggled his fingers forward in a signal to continue, then slowly inched forward in a crouch with the others evenly spaced out behind him.

"Thrik qua-na?"

One of the guards whispered in their strange language, lowering his spear and peering into the darkness in the general direction of the advancing warriors. He must have heard something rustle or spotted a bit of movement, but what alerted him didn't matter.

All seven warriors shot to their feet as one without any signal and charged the remaining distance, their confident steps muffled on the firm ground and voices silent. Three of them confronted the backpedaling sentries while Raldus led the rest straight into the tent where five more men were still scrambling from their cots, hands fervently searching for a weapon on the ground but already wearing their full armor. These were dispatched quickly, and since no alarm had gone up, all the warriors save Raldus sheathed their swords to gather whatever equipment they could lay their hands on.

Leaving them to their task, Raldus stepped back outside to see two of his men standing over four bodies laid out on the ground. After a quick glance to make sure no one else was coming, he finally sheathed his own sword and approached to see which one of his own people had fallen.

"Herius."

The single word, solemnly spoken, was all that was needed. Raldus gazed upon the body, honoring his fallen comrade with a moment of silence filled with gratitude for the man's service and sacrifice, then motioned for the others to pick him up and carry him away, the third lost in this effort to slow the enemy advance long enough for the capital to be evacuated.

When the others departed the tent, their outstretched arms laden down with armor and weapons, he sent them on their way, then pulled a set of flint and tinder from a pouch at his waist and struck it toward the tent. Two strikes was all it took to set the dry grass at its base smoking, and the fabric would follow soon enough.

Satisfied, he returned the tools to their pouch and walked away without a single glance behind him, not even when the night started to glow orange and shouts rose from further inside the camp.

Chapter Sixteen

Empty Victory

Two weeks of fighting every step of the way finally brought the Zaqulon army to their enemy's gates, but through it all Zishna Bujon refused to be deterred. After every attack by Naeran skirmishers, some of whom were now using armor stolen from the Zaqulon dead, the zishna cursed Triume Yalina and her insistence on delaying their attack, thus giving the savages time to organize.

It never should have taken this long to move the army up the Naeran road to their precious capital city, but at last Bujon stood looking at the metropolis stretched across both sides of the river. He was just as unimpressed with the sight now as the first time he saw it while scouting this land for his triume. Still, he supposed it had some notable features, such as the massive platform stretched out high over the river on which resided the main forum.

A remarkable achievement of engineering—for a bunch of savages.

"We're ready, Zishna," Neqar reported. Bujon opened his mouth to order the catapults to rain fire on the city, but closed it without uttering a word when his stomach suddenly tightened into a knot.

He peered ahead as he attuned all his senses toward his target and soon realized that something was indeed out of the ordinary.

It was too quiet. The only noises present were those of the birds and the rushing river some small distance to the west. No shouts from officers giving last-minute orders to the defending soldiers. No sound of horses snorting or whinnying as their riders prepared to ride out into battle. Not even the wail of a frightened child.

Even more telling was that there was also no movement to be seen, including on the riverbanks where he expected civilians to be gathering water to fight the coming fires.

"Bring my staff," Bujon muttered to Neqar who shot him a quizzical look before rushing off to obey.

The adjutant returned a few moments later and Bujon grabbed hold of his beam staff, feeling a sense of reassurance at the sensation of the warmth and soft vibration coursing through its shaft.

"I'm going up with First Corsa. Count thirty seconds, then follow with the second," he told Neqar emotionlessly.

"We're not attacking?" Neqar asked incredulously.

"Not yet."

The zishna set his jaw, then walked forward at the head of nearly five hundred men, setting a casual pace as they marched down the last stretch of road leading to the city's southern gate.

He gripped his staff ever tighter the closer they got to the city gate, watching for any sign of imminent attack, but nothing happened.

They made it all the way to the gate without seeing or hearing any sign of life on the walls above them. Not wanting to risk any of his men getting ambushed by sending them over to open the heavy wooden doors, he used his beam staff to slice through the center, and several soldiers ran up to throw them open the moment the beam dispersed.

"Victory!"

Dozens of soldiers yelled their battle cry as they ran around him into the city without having to be ordered, but he simply walked in as far as the center of the inside plaza where he rested his staff on the ground with a soft tap on the stone as he looked around in growing confusion.

When Neqar arrived, his soldiers followed the first to secure the plaza while the adjutant came up beside his zishna.

"Call up the entire army except the triume's guard. Spread out into the city. Find where they are hiding," Bujon ordered through gritted teeth.

It doesn't matter how clever you think you are. We will destroy you. One way or another.

Someone will answer for this mockery, Triume Jasud silently cursed all his enemies as he stood with Triume Yalina and their respective guard details. The musty scent of bricks still damp from that morning's storm entered his flared nostrils with each breath as he glared across the Naeran forum through the dim light filtered through an overcast sky.

To his left stood his lead agent, Zishna Bujon, who kept one hand on his sheathed sword while his greyish-blue eyes continued scanning the immediate area. Yalina was on his right, her formal posture resembling his own albeit more relaxed, and to her right stood her own lead agent, Avlana.

His musings were cut short when the pained and panicked screams of children crested the forum's eastern stairs with the promise of answers. First to appear at the top of the stairs were the midnight-blue helmets of over a dozen of their soldiers, followed by their masked faces before they came fully into view with a squealing Naeran brat dangling by the wrists between each pair.

"Such treatment is unnecessary," Yalina objected, speaking from the corner of her mouth in a tone only loud enough for her counterpart to discern.

"Your sympathy is wasted on them," Jasud dictated without caring if Bujon heard him.

"They are only children."

"Savage children. A low form of life unworthy of civilized treatment."

The group was close enough now to potentially overhear their conversation, mercifully forcing Yalina to refrain from arguing further.

The soldiers threw the six boys and three girls to the stones in front of the triumes, quickly forming a circle to prevent any escape before the prisoners could regain their footing and attempt an escape. All were barefoot and clad in filthy, torn clothes that barely resembled the tunics and dresses they once were. None of them were above the age of ten years while the youngest couldn't be any older than five.

Jasud yearned to personally wrest from these urchins the answers he sought, but refused to degrade himself by having his voice heard in their presence, so he signaled Bujon with a short nod who then stepped forward to tower over the wide-eyed, filthy creatures.

"Why is this city empty?" the zishna asked in the Naeran language, his voice booming like that of a thespian projecting his voice.

The oldest of the boys stared back with defiance burning in his blue eyes while the rest looked around at their captors with fresh tears flowing into the tracks in their dirty faces.

"Where have they gone?"

If they knew the answer, none of the trembling children had the courage to speak it.

"Tell me!" Bujon roared.

This outburst sent all but the oldest scrambling backward only to be fiercely kicked forward again by the soldiers.

A movement from his right drew Jasud's gaze to Avlana who had stepped forward and was now removing her helmet, revealing her tightly bound dark red hair. Jasud glared at Yalina from the corner of his eyes in a signal to stop this foolishness, but his counterpart's own expression remained infuriatingly passive.

Avlana inserted herself between Bujon and the oldest boy, the former's eyes boring into the back of her head while the latter's darted from side to side as if alert for some trickery. The female agent knelt while pulling down her mask and looked the child directly in the eyes as she spoke.

"Everyone else has gone. Why are you still here?" she questioned in a motherly tone. The boy's body shook and lip quivered as he did his best to hold on to whatever reason was preventing him from speaking, but he could not resist the woman's charm.

"They don't like us. Sometimes they hurt us. We hid."

"Where did they go?"

"We don't know."

"Why did they leave?"

"We don't know!"

"Leave him alone!" another boy shouted, earning him a backhand from a soldier that sent him sprawling to the pavement.

Avlana glared at the soldier, disapproval burning in her blue eyes, but even she knew better than to speak against her own kind in the presence of savages.

She looked back at the one to whom she had been speaking, then stood and smiled down at him.

"I believe you," she said with a smile, then replaced her mask and helmet before turning to Yalina to deliver her report in their own language.

"These boys are nothing but street urchins left behind when the city was evacuated. We're not going to learn anything from them."

The last line was delivered while looking at Bujon who glared back with fury burning in his greyish eyes between helmet and mask.

Yalina accepted the report with a nod, Avalana resumed her place at her side, and Jasud gave a similar nod to Bujon who ordered the soldiers to take the boys away, each of his words heavy with disgust.

"Treachery!" Triume Jasud shouted the moment he was sure the soldiers and their charges were out of earshot down the stairs, releasing all the rage built up on his passage through the empty city and interrogation of the children.

"Is it treachery to not want to die?" Triume Yalina questioned, her tone betraying her own confusion despite the challenge in her question. At least she didn't make a ridiculous remark about him needing to control himself in front of the soldiers guarding the stairs.

"Cowardice, then," he grumbled as he looked around. He looked off toward the large statue in the forum's center with the low wall around it and considered ordering Bujon to blast the fictitious idol apart with a beam staff.

In their search of the city, the soldiers had also discovered that not only were the city's inhabitants gone, but so too were the majority of its supplies of food and military equipment.

"Where did they go, and what do they hope to achieve with this?" Yalina wondered aloud.

"Find them!" Jasud barked at no one in particular.

"I'll take care of it personally, Honored One," Bujon promised, then gave the triumes a short bow before hurrying off.

"They will not escape us," Jasud muttered for Yalina's ears alone.

"It is good that we did not have to fight here. None of our people had to die, nor do we have to repair the city before we can put it to its full use," she suggested optimistically.

He didn't respond, but instead stormed off toward the senate building on the east bank. Perhaps he could find something there to give him insight into the minds of these savages who were clearly incapable of acting logically.

The setting sun peeked from beneath the clouds to cast an eerie glow over the road leading through Izagion's main gate as the latest legion to arrive passed through. Raldus watched from above, once again clad in his armor from the monastery, the polished steel shining in the evening light and drawing the gaze of the legionnaires who held aloft their spears in salute to their champion.

Nearly the entire military of the Naeran Republic was gathered here or within days of arriving while only token garrisons remained to maintain order in those cities still free. Many citizens had also come here for shelter, but most were spread out among those cities and towns not in the invader's path. He could only hope that he, the legate, and others were right in their belief that the invaders would choose to pursue and attack here before going after anything else. If they were wrong, there would be no stopping these people from completely overrunning the land.

These thoughts inevitably led to his new home at Our Sacred Refuge, and he looked to the southwest as he considered how the monks and townspeople were faring with their current guests, the sick and injured who most needed a safe place to recover. He may be a stubborn old man intent on remaining isolated from the world, but Abbot Jerald would no doubt provide the best of care to all the people under his charge and keep them safe if at all possible.

Most of all, he thought of the woman who saved him from the brink of death and refused to give up on him to once again save him from the darkness weighing upon his soul, then agreed to become his wife to forever be at his side. She should be giving birth to their firstborn any day now, and how he longed to be there with her. He deeply wished to hold her close while running his fingers through her dark hair, but the best thing he could do for her and their child now was to ensure a world where at least the possibility of peace and safety existed.

A horn blast from beside him drew his attention back to his immediate surroundings, and he glanced down to see that the road below was now empty amid the failing light. The gate mechanism groaned beneath him, and the heavy stone doors slowly swung shut, sealing the city against any horrors that might threaten the people inside.

When a resounding thud followed by silence broken only by the gusting of a gentle breeze indicated the doors were secure, Raldus nodded to the guardsmen atop the gate with him then headed down into the city to begin the task of assigning the new arrivals to their defensive positions.

It would not take the enemy long to find them, making every second of time until then a precious gem needed to buy their best chance at survival.

"You have discovered where the savages of this city have fled?" Zishna Bujon irritably demanded of the two scouts standing below him on the floor of Naera's senate chamber.

The triumes were kind enough to assign this space to him as his office while they took up residence in the consul's mansion, and even though it was a primitive design, it was nice to be conducting business in a building constructed for that purpose instead of in a tent or out in the open.

It was now five days after finding this city empty, during which time they'd learned nothing of its former inhabitants, and he'd begun to doubt they would find anything. Even though he'd been told these two had tracked the natives, he was not yet ready to get his hopes up and made no attempt to shield his waning patience.

"Yes, Zishna. They have taken all their remaining forces to Heshilon, fortifying both the city and nearby fort in preparation for a siege."

"Their filth never should have been allowed to contaminate ground broken by our ancestors. You are sure of this?"

"We have seen this with our own eyes, Zishna."

The news finally brought a grin to Bujon's face as he leaned forward in the chair mounted on the chamber's center dais to deliver his next words.

"Not even walls built by our people's own hands shall shelter them for long. We march at once to wipe out this pitiful attempt at resistance. When they are gone, nothing will stand in the way of us asserting dominance over the rest of this land."

A teenage girl took the bundle of freshly laundered clothes from Ariela's arms the moment she stepped into the monastery's dining hall, allowing her to slowly but surely make her way to the first bed in the improvised ward, both hands resting on her swollen belly.

"How are you feeling today?" she asked the blonde-haired young man as she lowered herself to the stool at his bedside.

"Better," he rasped.

She laid a hand on his forehead, noting the improved color in the soldier's cheeks and smiling when the skin proved cool to the touch.

Though the smile remained, a certain sadness welled up inside her at the memory of another man she'd nursed back to health not that long ago. Oh, how she longed to be near him now, except that it had better not be in the manner she was currently by this one.

"Your fever is gone. It won't be long before you're fully healed," she assured the wounded man.

She stood up to move on to her next patient, but a sudden, sharp pain shooting through her entire body set her to leaning against the bed to keep from collapsing.

"Are you alright?" the bed's occupant asked as he looked up at her, his brow creased in concern. She tried to answer, but it was all she could do to keep from crying out in pain.

An older woman in the room noticed her and rushed over, steadying her with one hand on her shoulder while placing the other on her belly. Tania took one look in Ariela's eyes, then turned her toward the entrance while waving over other women in the room. Once outside, they turned her toward her home, and Tania was quick to shut down her protests squeezed through gritted teeth.

"Today, you are the patient."

Chapter Seventeen

Tangled Webs

"It is an odd sensation to find wisdom where you were sure there was none," Triume Yalina remarked to her lead agent, Avlana.

"This shows they value their people above their possessions," Avlana agreed, glancing to the north at their enemy's final refuge.

The two of them were seated outside Yalina's personal tent, a large collection of thick blue fabric inside of which were many sections designed to mimic the comforts of the triume temple, no matter where its resident may find herself. Although they were far from any potential danger, Avlana insisted on wearing her armor instead of her agent's robes, her only concession for comfort being to set her helmet on the ground between her feet and to leave her mask pulled down. Of course, Yalina wore the traditional robes of her office, although she had traded the soft shoes for a sturdier pair more suited to these wild lands, and her long white hair was comfortably draped over the back of her chair.

Only four other agents were present, standing guard around the table and chairs in full armor as the triume enjoyed some afternoon refreshments with her friend as a pleasant breeze kept them cool.

Among the many trees north of them were camped approximately eighty-thousand of their soldiers, nearly their entire remaining army.

Only a few thousand men were left behind to watch over the cities and forts over which they had assumed control.

Zishna Bujon had wanted to use the beam staffs to burn down those trees to make space for the camp, but in a rare display of restraint, Triume Jasud ordered him to leave them alone amid concerns the crystals powering the weapons were losing their charge.

Out of sight beyond the woods waited a far larger Naeran force composed of multiple legions. The Zaqulons did not know the exact number arrayed against them, but it was at least twice as many which they had fielded and probably more.

The defenders were stretched out between their naval fort and the city to its west, which the locals called Izagion but was known as Heshilon to the Zaqulons. The irony of the situation was not lost on Yalina, as the walls which their enemy now hoped would protect them were built by the very ones seeking their destruction. Their ancestors once sought to colonize this land long before anyone else arrived, and Heshilon was to be a new sister city to Zaqulon, but too few people were willing to leave their home at the time and the government was forced to abandon the project.

Those who came later sought protection behind the massive walls and housed their leaders in the palace, the only structures constructed before the Zaqulons vacated the site. The settlers built the rest of the city themselves, most of which was hidden behind the walls, and Yalina shuddered when she imagined those ugly, primitive structures next to the great works of her ancestors.

Now the city's current inhabitants stood side-by-side with the Naerans against its rightful owners, a choice borne either from ego or terror.

"Find Jasud and relay my desire to speak with him immediately," Yalina commanded at the conclusion of the small meal. Avlana snatched up her helmet and rose from her seat in one fluid motion, executed a short bow, then set out to find the other triume likely hanging around their army's front line.

When their scouts reported on the location of the Naeran army while they were still in Naera, Yalina had sent a message back to Zaqulon asking Vejalon for his opinion on a proposal she was considering. His response came while they were on the march, and it was time to inform the remaining member of the triumvirate.

"You want to negotiate with them?" Triume Jasud questioned. What Yalina had just finished telling him sounded like something Vejalon would suggest, but he thought she was wiser than that young fool.

"Yes. This shift in their tactics suggests they may yet discover a means of fighting us. We can still defeat them here, but only at great cost, and that will leave us vulnerable to a possible counter-strategy that could extend this war beyond our ability to fight it," Yalina argued.

"Your fear and doubt already cost us precious time once, and now you want to risk losing everything?"

"These people clearly are not as foolish as we considered. There may yet be a way we can coexist with them. We should make an effort to determine this while we yet hold the advantage."

"No! They are fit only to be destroyed, and we do it now!"

"The decision has been made," Yalina stated with infuriating calm as she handed him the paper she'd been holding the whole time.

He yanked it out of her hand and looked down at it, noticing first the official seal of the triumvirate at the top, then reading the statement supporting Yalina's proposal, and finally recognizing Vejalon's signature and seal at the bottom.

So the little cretin was involved in this after all.

"We will not stop," he stated matter-of-factly as he threw the paper back at her, then turned and stomped away as it floated to the ground.

"You are outvoted and cannot act alone!" she shouted after him, but he did not respond.

"We already control most of this land. Do you suppose it's enough?" Bujon asked the officer walking beside him as he inspected the man's soldiers in his capacity as the army commander. As officers, neither wore a mask to ensure the clarity of spoken orders, but were otherwise in full armor which included their helmets with white plumes of synthetic fiber.

"Absolutely not. Our people's survival depends on gaining as many resources as possible," the officer declared.

"Our current gains could support our population and more for centuries."

"Is this the word of the triumvirate?"

"I am not speaking for the triumvirate or any one of the triumes. I desire to know your thoughts."

"Then I say it is not enough. Even if it were, we should at least reclaim the city founded by our ancestors. It's insulting what these savages have done with it."

Bujon nodded thoughtfully, betraying no emotion even as his heart swelled in his chest. Such was the sentiment of every officer to whom he had talked since Triume Jasud returned from his meeting with Triume Yalina, assuring him that they knew what must be done as well as he did.

"Your soldiers feel the same?"

"They do, Zishna."

"Make sure of it, no matter what happens," he demanded.

As suggested by his father and the legate, and further approved by Keid later, Raldus rode among the soldiers atop the most magnificent steed they could find, a white beast with rippling muscles that practically towered over any other horse. A red plume of horsehair running front to back was added to his helmet to further set him apart from the other officers, and his steel breastplate shone so brightly in the sun that even the invaders must be able to see it in the distance.

The red was a controversial choice for everyone but the legate who had learned enough to understand its meaning. For anyone in the government or army to support such a decision which broke from the traditions of their people came as a huge surprise to Raldus, but it was a welcome one. Everyone else wanted him to use blue, with the consul even suggesting he take a new helmet from the consularians, but he refused on the grounds that color represented the sky god Keslu, a deity in whom he no longer believed. Red made sense not only because it represented Raldus' faith in Rosjen, symbolizing the blood he shed for all people, but also because no one else wore that color, thus further setting him apart as the republic's champion.

All who saw him perked up, and many even cheered as every morning since the army arrived at Izagion he rode from the city's walls, through the legions stretched between it and Fort Aquasvigilate to the east, and finally to the fort itself before turning back. Each day he chose a different route, calling out greetings to anyone he recognized, no matter how well he knew them, and waving to all those who waved or called out to him.

Over two-hundred thousand men were gathered here, nearly everything the republic could field without overly weakening its defenses elsewhere. This was too many to efficiently place in the fort, city, or between them, so around fifty-thousand were sent over the bridge to the other side of the lake to function as reserves and to make sure the wild tribes didn't take the opportunity to cause further trouble despite their own weakened state. Raldus had ridden among this reserve force that first day since they were just as important as anyone else, but had stuck to the forward positions since then as it took too much time to ride that far out and back over Lake Speigudel.

In addition to all of this, two dozen galleys floated on the calm, clear water as close to the shore as their drafts would allow, each one recently fitted with either a catapult or ballista. When the fighting started, they would launch their projectiles over the Naeran formations to rain down on the invaders, and their archers would also prove invaluable should either the city or fort be taken in the fighting. Raldus had suggested they also place at least one galley in the river between the city and fort, tying it to the bridge to hold it against the current, but Tullus decided against it for fear of the enemy using a beam weapon to set it afire and possibly prevent them from sending other boats downriver if needed.

On the third day of the invaders' arrival, he finished his rounds by mid-morning and trotted back into Izagion under the eyes of steel-armored legionnaires and linen-protected city guard manning the walls, and dismounted in the gate plaza in front of Mettius and Tullus.

"Why do they wait?" Legate Tullus asked as the champion passed the reins to a teenage boy who then led the horse away for some well-deserved feeding and grooming.

"There's no way to know. I don't see them digging ditches, building fences, or anything of the like. They aren't even sending out sorties to test our defenses," Raldus reported as he undid his helmet strap and removed the heavy hunk of metal with its plume to hold it under his right arm.

"They're just sitting and watching?" Mettius questioned.

"So it would seem."

"Very peculiar," Tullus intoned.

"They could be trying to get us to attack them, to draw our forces into the open where they can be destroyed before they assault the city walls," Mettius suggested.

"We should indulge them. We have the numbers to surround and overwhelm them, especially in an unfortified position," Tullus proposed.

"I would agree, but I don't think that is what is going on here," Raldus disagreed.

"Why?" Tullus asked.

"Something doesn't feel right. Until now, the invaders have used fear as their biggest weapon, but now it's as if *they're* afraid."

"All the more reason to attack and press our advantage."

"It's tempting, but our biggest advantage is in Izagion's walls. Our best chance at surviving this lies in using them alongside our numbers. Supplies in the city and fort alone ensure that we can hold for months if needed, and continued access to the coast via the river means we can keep this up for as long as it takes."

"Didn't you say that they did something similar at Fort Nelius? They clearly weren't afraid then," Mettius interjected.

"And they only had a tenth of the numbers they do now," Tullus added.

"That's true, but we inflicted a great deal of damage on them, perhaps more than they expected."

"That could be the reason for their hesitation now," Mettius mused.

"You're the champion. The army will follow your lead, and I trust you. What is your decision?" Tullus concluded.

"We wait."

"You are out of order!" Triume Yalina censored Triume Jasud in the open space between their two tents. Such an outburst was improper even if only agents were around to witness it, but the circumstances warranted doing away with appearances. Five of Jasud's agents stood on either side of him, including Zishna Bujon, while Avlana and the other four of Yalina's agents mirrored them on her side. Not a single muscle twitched as these elite guards glared across the small space between them, eyes between masks and helmet brim hardened and alert for any signs of treachery.

"No one may leave the camp without Triume Jasud's express permission," Bujon declared, his expression cold and hard.

"How dare you speak to an Honored One out of turn," Avlana confronted as she took a step forward. Yalina stopped her with an outstretched arm, and the agent dutifully stepped back into place.

"My agents were acting on the will of the triumvirate," Yalina clarified in a voice strained from tightly controlled calm.

"That was not our understanding."

The triume suppressed a sigh, then raised an eyebrow to her counterpart to get him to chime in.

"What has been set in motion cannot be stopped, and I see no reason to make such an attempt," Jasud responded with a gleeful smile.

"You cannot defy a majority vote of the triumvirate, and how dare your agents block mine from carrying out my orders!"

"*I* have earned the loyalty of this army! They will obey *me*, no matter what you and that fool Vejalon say!" Jasud countered, punctuating his points with a jab of his finger at his chest then at her.

"We stand with you, Honored One," Bujon confirmed with a smirk.

"This is treason," Yalina threatened, her low tone prompting her agents to move a hand to the hilt of their blades. The opposing agents did not reciprocate, and the action only served to broaden the zishna's grin.

"Perhaps, but there isn't anything you can do about it," Jasud challenged.

"It wasn't only his agents that stood in our way, Eminence. There were also soldiers helping them," Avlana disclosed.

"There is no doubt there are those who would support you, but most are eager for victory. The only means for you to get this army to stand down is by fighting your own people, and where will that leave us?" Bujon interjected.

"Again you speak to an honored triume with disrespect," Avlana hissed as she slid her sword partway from its leather sheath.

Yalina placed a hand on the back of her friend's neck and squeezed on the soft fabric of her underarmor, bidding the agent to return to a less threatening stature with the simple gesture.

When she looked back at Jasud, she saw him watching the scene with childlike glee dancing within his blue eyes, and when he met her gaze, he broke out into a grin at the realization of his victory.

"You can sit back and watch us seize our destiny. Do not attempt to interfere again," Jasud decreed, then turned with a swirl of his robes and walked away with four of his agents following. Bujon held back long enough to give Yalina and her agents a pointed look, his gaze lingering on Avlana a moment longer than the others, then he also followed his triume.

Her thoughts raced as Yalina fought to come up with something that would get them to see reason while they were still within the sound of her voice, but then her whole body slumped in place when she realized there was nothing, and she stood there with head down as her agents closed in to set reassuring hands on her arms and shoulders.

Their people were committed to this course and to whatever end it brought them.

Chapter Eighteen

All or Nothing

The first rays of dawn dispersed through the mist rising from the gently flowing river to shroud the field in front of the city.

From within the softly illumined fog, hundreds of shadowy human forms took shape as Legate Tullus peered out from atop Izagion's main gate.

"It's about time," he mumbled, his head slowly panning to the left as he took in the assembled enemy formation. After all the senseless waiting, he was actually somewhat pleased when a messenger roused him in the predawn hours to report considerable movement inside the invader's camp as reported by a scout runner.

It would not be long now before the battle was joined under the growing light.

"Where are their shields?" Karsin, captain of the Izagion guard as marked by the red coat of arms on his grey linen armor, wondered aloud as he peered at the lines of blue-armored soldiers from the legate's right side.

"They don't need them," Tullus quietly responded."What about cavalry?"

"They don't use them."

The leadership of the city's guard garrison was fully briefed on the foe they faced, so why was this man asking foolish questions now?

"And yours?"

The legate looked away from his counterpart and bit his lower lip, then calmly explained the strategy all over again.

"Our only advantage is in making them come to us. It is suicide to sortie against them."

It occurred to Tullus that the man's ignorance shouldn't come as a surprise given that it had been centuries since his people had to fight a real war, having enjoyed the republic's protection from their northern and eastern neighbors in that time.

The rhythmic thudding from thousands of feet striking the ground in perfect unison drew everyone's gaze to the east, but none were able to see any further than the river through the lingering fog. Those figures which were visible in front of them remained still as statues, which they could be for all the watchers knew, while the pace of the unseen marchers steadily increased.

"They're only going after the fort?" Karsin breathed, his voice low as if fearing to draw the attention of the attackers.

"They don't have the numbers to attack both the city and fort at the same time, and the walls of the fort are much easier to breach than those of the city."

The sounds of marching morphed into those of a full-on charge across the soft ground, and now the men at the gate could see the mists swirling around a dark mass deep within as the dawning sun gradually shone more light upon the spectacle. As Tullus watched, his visage formed into a grim smile at the sight of those arrogant fools, a vision made complete by his imagination and knowledge of the terrain.

A low rumble rose to permeate the scene, and suddenly the thunder of armored soldiers charging across a field was replaced with alarmed shouts as men fell into the hidden trench the defenders had prepared for them, now exposed to swallow them up.

When a faint shout rose from the direction of the fort, Tullus glanced in its direction in time to behold flickering, yellowish tendrils shoot out and arc down toward the trap. The fog instantly blazed bright orange as screams of agony and panicked cries split the air.

Though the fog was now burning away in the intense heat sent out by the flaming oil set ablaze around the attackers, smoke poured forth to replace it, proving to be a small mercy to those watching when the sights remained hidden. Tullus only wished he could also stop up his ears against the cries of agony rising up from those poor creatures as though the underworld itself had opened up to sound forth the screams of its tortured souls, but such an action was unbecoming in the sight of his men.

They may be butchers invading his land, but no one deserved to be burned alive.

"By the gods," Karsin breathed. Tullus glanced at him to see him watching the spectacle with mouth hanging open as the faint orange light of the distant flames danced upon his face. He next looked through the thinning fog at those enemy troops still assembled on the field before the city itself, many of whom had broken ranks with the intent to rush to the aid of their brethren, but were now being shoved back into place by their unmasked officers designated by white helmet plumes.

"There will be no more fighting today," Tullus quietly concluded before turning away and descending the steps into the city.

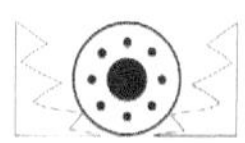

"They will not be turned back so easily today," Mettius mused as his mount snorted and kicked at the dirt.

"Yesterday, they faced fire. Today, they face the spears and swords of Naeran cavalrymen," the tribune to his right declared.

"If we are called," Mettius muttered, earning himself a hateful look from his army counterpart.

To give all their units the best chance of success, not to mention survival, Raldus had spread the twelve Stoneforge Warriors between the fort, city, and defensive line between the two. As the most experienced among them, Mettius was put with the cavalry assigned to reinforce any breaches in the line. The horsemen would then push back the attackers so their own infantry could plug the gap or serve as a rear guard in the event of a retreat.

So far, the only action he had taken was to contend with this young fool.

"Who ever heard of a Stoneforge Warrior on a horse anyway?" the tribune remarked with a tilt of his head toward the prime on his other side, smiling upon hearing the mocking snickers he sought.

"The warriors of Stoneforge are trained in all forms of combat," Mettius responded coolly.

"Pfft. Training is no substitute for experience."

"I have experienced far more than you can imagine, boy."

The elder warrior's horse shook its head and pawed at the dirt, causing him to tighten his grip on the reins to keep the agitated beast from taking off.

"Careful, old man. He's a spirited one, and I don't want to have to chase after you."

More snickers from the other soldiers.

Time to put all of these arrogant punks in their place, Mettius thought to himself just before laughing out loud.

"What's so funny?"

"I was thinking about training my son. He always thought he knew everything too, but he still learned respect. I believe you know him? The man leading this army? One of the few men to be named champion of the republic while still breathing, and the first to receive that honor at such a young age?"

Silence.

From the corner of his eye, Mettius observed the tribune hunched over and chewing the inside of his lower lip while the others found something else to hold their attention. It was a rather satisfying sight, but he did not press his advantage or even so much as smile as he looked back toward the enemy camp at the edge of sight across the empty field halved by the cloudy waters of the relatively narrow river.

Their abilities—and honor—would be tested in battle soon enough.

Two days of relentless siege had left every muscle, bone, and joint in Raldus' body screaming with pain and fatigue, and he could barely breathe in the thick smoke hugging the ground in the thick air as flaming jars continued to rain down around him, but he spared no thought for rest.

The situation would be considerably improved if they destroyed the enemy siege weapons, but they were well-protected from counter-attack and far outside the range of their own catapults and ballistae.

One more in a long list of advantages the invaders held over the Naeran legions.

"I've had enough of you!" Raldus vented his frustration as an enemy charged down the top of the fort's wall toward him, screaming as he came.

He allowed his opponent to strike a glancing blow against his shield, then leaned in with his shoulder to trap the man's sword against his own gut. Metal clanged as Raldus pressed the flat of his blade against the soldier's other arm, pinning it to his side, after which he leaned into the shield with all his weight and drove the man to the wall's edge.

The invader tripped over the raised edge and Raldus opened his arms to let him fall screaming into the mass of his comrades swirling around the rope ladders.

He took no time to savor his triumph and spun around to face whatever came next.

"They're coming over the walls!"

Raldus looked down the line to see a group of blue-armored soldiers pushing against legionnaires as they backpedaled in a desperate attempt to create the space they needed to counterattack.

He spotted a similar sight when he glanced over his shoulder which meant the walls were lost—for now.

"Fall back!" he commanded. If they could regroup behind the walls, then the fort might still be saved to fight another day.

The cry was taken up by the officers, echoing down the length of the wall and out of earshot as it passed from one sector to the next.

Raldus ran to the top of the nearest set of stairs leading down into the fort, then spun around and kept watch with raised sword and shield, battered as it was, while sweat and blood laden defenders rushed past him.

As increasing numbers of invaders swarmed onto the wall, the volleys of flaming jars flying into the fort ceased. The fires gutting the fort still burned, but at least this gave the defenders more room to maneuver without having to worry about one of those things smashing upon their heads and setting them alight at any given moment.

An invader grabbed one of the retreating defenders from behind, causing the legionnaire to scream when his head was pulled back to expose his neck to a sword poised to strike, but Raldus thrust his own blade past the man's head and into the neck of his attacker.

He swung his shield behind the legionnaire to prop him up until he could regain his balance after the enemy fell to the stone bricks, then followed him down the stairs when it was clear only enemies remained behind.

Scores of blue-armored invaders chased after them, quickly breaking through the second defensive line and forcing the defenders to execute a fighting withdrawal deeper into the fort.

In a street near the center of the smoke-filled complex, Raldus hastily organized a shield wall, lining up the men into a square two lines deep which parted only to allow in other retreating legionnaires. Then he spotted the centurion in charge of the eastern wall and pulled him aside for an update.

"They've broken through. We couldn't hold them," the man gasped, his dark eyes darting around at the chaos surrounding them.

"No one from the western wall is here," Raldus mused, silently concluding that the entrenched defenders between the fort and city must still be holding.

"These will be attacking them from behind soon enough."

A legionnaire fell backward into Raldus who barely noticed him in time to move the point of his sword aside.

He shoved the man back to his feet, then grabbed his shoulder and spun him around, resulting in a sword pointed at his gut before the man realized they were on the same side.

"Run to the western wall. Tell them to fall back to the northern flank."

The poor, exhausted soul started to apologize for pointing a weapon at his champion, but Raldus cut him off.

"Hurry!" he demanded with a shove.

This time the man, scarcely old enough to be serving in battle, did as he was told, nearly tripping over his own feet before steadying himself and pushing through his fellow defenders to carry out his task.

"Pull them back," Raldus ordered the centurion, then shouted for all to hear, "To the north! All Naerans to the north wall!"

Those holding the north side of the square ran off immediately, opening it for those behind to follow between flaming buildings on streets clear of invaders for the moment, but the other three sides stood their ground.

"What are you doing?!" Raldus demanded of the centurion, pulling him back when he went to join those at the southern flank.

"Get out of here! We'll slow them down long enough for you to reassemble!"

It was an awful thing to leave men behind to die, but victory and survival for the whole often required such sacrifices.

Fortunately, in this case Raldus' idea meant these men didn't have to linger long enough for all to meet their end.

"I have a plan. It needs only seconds to implement. Once I am out of sight, you must follow."

The two locked eyes, the centurion nodded his understanding, and Raldus ran off without awaiting another word or signal.

His legs felt like supple leather, but he ran as fast as they would carry him, putting the screams of pain and death from his mind and heart as the din of battle gradually faded behind him. Many who preceded him aided their brothers with arms linked over their shoulders as they limped to safety together. Others called out to him as he passed, having succumbed to their fatigue or wounds and collapsed to the dirt, but he ignored them.

Any delay now could mean death for them all.

"This day may see the end of this war," Triume Jasud murmured. He smirked as he dismissed the messenger with a casual wave, then leaned back in his chair to gaze up at the smoke streaming into the sky.

Closing his eyes, he imagined his soldiers sweeping over the walls of the primitive fort in a purifying wave of deep blue shining with the light of their people.

The walls of the city would not be breached so easily, but once this bastion of savages fell, it was only a matter of time before all of those stubborn fools were put to the sword. They might even come to see reason at last and surrender, choosing servitude over certain death.

It was all thanks to him, ensuring that he would be remembered long after he was gone. The savages might even worship him as a god after this, which was a pleasant thought indeed.

Bounding up the steps for the northern wall two at a time, Raldus rushed up to the two men in simple leather armor beside a pole twice their height from which five flags of different shapes and colors fluttered in the wind.

"Signal the fleet," he gasped before his voice gave out. He drew a long breath through both nose and mouth, grateful for the relatively clear air on this flank, then swallowed and finished his order.

"Unleash hell. On the fort."

Both men glanced at each other, then at their champion, eyes wide with disbelief.

Not having enough air to chastise them, Raldus took each by a shoulder and shoved them toward the pole to demonstrate his sincerity.

Once they were arranging the flags to relay the order to the galleys waiting in the lake beyond, Raldus turned and looked down as the rest of the beleaguered defenders from the other walls made their way to relative safety. His body screamed for him to lie down, and he was tempted to at least lean over with hands on knees as he caught his breath, but he did neither of these things and stubbornly stood tall to give a sight from which his men could gather courage.

"It's done, Champion."

Raldus nodded solemnly at the report from the signalman, then breathed a sigh of relief when he spotted the centurion striding up to their line with less than a third of those who'd covered the withdrawal.

It was a small comfort to know that he wouldn't be raining down fire on his own men.

The twang of dozens of ropes releasing split the air, and he looked up to see flaming arrows, ballista bolts, and balls of fire arcing overhead before crashing down into the fort.

Those few buildings not already alight from the attacks of the invaders would soon join the rest under this new onslaught, but that was of little consequence as long as the walls held. They must deny the invaders this victory for as long as possible.

"Push on! Give them no time to breathe!" Zishna Bujon galvanized his men.

He spotted one sitting on a doorstep, hanging his head while leaning on his spear and stomped up to shove him into the dust.

"No rest until the fort is ours!" he growled when the man looked up at him with eyes wide and mouth agape.

"But it *is* ours," the soldier whined, then crawled backward when his superior advanced on him.

"Do savages yet live inside these walls?"

"I, I, I..."

"The answer is yes, which means that our work is not done."

The soldier scrambled to his feet under the zishna's brutal glare, and finally rushed off after his comrades headed to the north.

Bujon glanced around and spotted another one of his men standing there staring into the sky. Grumbling under his breath, he strode up to give the lazy wretch a piece of his mind, but the soldier heard him coming and spoke first.

"Did you hear something?"

The almost casual wonder in the man's voice halted the zishna in his tracks. In an instant, the man's expression changed from simple curiosity to absolute terror, and Bujon followed his gaze to the northern sky.

An obscenity formed on his lips as dozens of fireballs trailing black smoke amid hundreds of flaming arrows arced down toward them, but the projectiles struck before he got it all out. Thundering bursts ripped through the air as the ground shook from the impact, and it was all Bujon could do to keep his balance as he danced about on the quaking street.

He glanced back at the soldier, who now lay on his back with an arrow sticking out of his face, then at the sky again as more fire fell toward him.

A nearby building exploded, sending Bujon diving to the ground where he covered his head as splinters of wood pelted all around and a cloud of dust enveloped him.

When he looked up, he was confronted with the sight of throngs of his own soldiers tripping over each other as they fled the horrors raining down on them.

"Run!"

"Save yourselves!"

"We're all going to die!"

Such were their shouts as they gave in to fear, which only served to set fire to Bujon's blood as he launched to his feet.

"No! Push forward! Get close to them!" he screamed to no avail.

He grabbed one young man by the shoulders and pulled him close to shout in his face.

"Keep fighting!"

"Let me go," the boy whimpered.

Bujon backhanded him across the face, ignoring the pain from striking the helmet guard, but was interrupted from chastising him further by a wave of heat washing over them followed by wails of pain.

Both looked toward the source, and Bujon's limbs went numb at the sight of three Zaqulon soldiers engulfed in flames as they flailed about.

The boy wriggled out of his arms and ran away as he stood there, unable to move or speak as he watched those men burn and fall to the ground, their cries ripping apart his soul.

A sudden silence broke his stupor and he looked up to learn that the volleys had ceased, but then fresh shouts erupted which brought his gaze back down as Naeran legionnaires charged out of the smoky shadows.

With no other choice left to him, Bujon turned and ran.

A zishna in the Zaqulon army; agent to the oldest triume, ran from a horde of savages.

"Impossible!" Jasud roared at the messenger's report. He leapt from his couch, barreled through the tent flaps, and balled his hands into fists at his sides as he peered at the fresh smoke darkening the sky to the north.

He stalked off toward the forward command post, grinding his teeth and grumbling under his breath as he walked. All those who saw him gave him a wide berth, fearfully bowing as they backed up, but he neither noticed nor cared.

The first thing he observed after climbing the hill to the white cloth pavilion was Yalina, guarded by three agents, her arms dangling at her sides as the breeze swirled her dark robes with diamond trim about her while her waist-length, braided white hair remained motionless above the flapping fabric.

She said nothing when he came up beside her to glare at the fort in the distance, scowling at the sight of his soldiers running back across the field toward them.

"Fools! Cowards! How can they run from savages?" he hissed.

"How long will you continue underestimating these people?" Yalina challenged, but he ignored the accusation.

"The fort was conquered. How did this happen?"

She turned to face him, and waited for him to meet her amber gaze before speaking.

"You failed them. You failed us all. That's what happened."

She held his gaze in the iron grip of her own, daring him to refute her, then brushed past him and stalked off with her agents trailing when he did not.

"Ludicrous," he mumbled once she was gone.

The fleeing soldiers were now reaching the camp, so he descended the hill, determined to find answers for this travesty.

Both triumes listened patiently as the sweat and filth covered Bujon Hannir relayed the story of how they pushed the Naerans in their fort all the way to the north wall where they expected to finish them. Then he told them it was as if the gods of the primitives unleashed their fury upon the Zaqulons: raining fire, stone, and arrows down upon them.

He insisted they did not flee in fear, but rather from the knowledge there was nothing they could do against this onslaught. Only their deaths would be achieved, which would prove a devastating blow to their already small army.

As the zishna spoke, Jasud sat with both arms laid on the rests of his chair, his hands tightly gripping the ends and turning the knuckles white. Although she felt a certain satisfaction at seeing both of these arrogant men humbled, Yalina chose a relaxed posture with hands folded in her lap so as to offer a sense of safety to the man before her. It would not be wise to foster dissension between the triumes and the commander of their army, especially given the previous confrontation between herself and this man.

When he finished, Jasud dismissed the man, then rose to pace on the thick, purple rug covering the dirt between the tent's canvas walls. Her only action was to watch him while doing her best to suppress a triumphant smile at his shattered ego.

"We should have destroyed those boats at the start of the battle," he complained.

"It was discussed, and we all agreed that it is not within our means."

"We are Zaqulons! Nothing is outside our means!" he roared from the center of the throne tent, then resumed his pacing when she did not retaliate.

Only their agents were close enough outside to hear this outburst, which should never have happened even in their hearing, but it was unlikely to shatter their image with them as it would a commoner.

"Enemy soldiers prevent us from getting close enough on land to use our staffs, and boat building is beyond the scope of our engineers."

"Their lack of knowledge weakens us all."

"There is no surface water in Zaqulon. Our people have never needed boats before, and we did not see the need to learn for this campaign. Do not blame them for *your* failure to determine all ends," Yalina denounced harshly.

He whirled toward her, blue eyes flashing with anger, but she calmly stared back until he turned away to face the tent wall.

"These savages cannot resist us forever. We will destroy them."

With that, Jasud marched out of the tent, leaving Yalina to look after him with sadness threatening to overwhelm her.

Which of us is going to be destroyed?

When this war began, there was no doubt as to the outcome, making such a question unthinkable to even be asked.

Now, she wasn't so sure. Perhaps if they negotiated a settlement with the Naerans, both sides would prosper, but Jasud had seen to it that was no longer a possibility.

The only thing she could do now was wait and see how it all turned out.

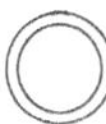

The fires were out, but smoke continued trailing up to the darkening sky as Keid entered the fort. He acknowledged his escort with a nod when the young man reassured him that it was perfectly safe and tried not to weep as he looked around at the destruction.

All of the buildings he encountered were burnt-out husks with collapsed roofs and gaps in the concrete walls. None looked habitable, a theory confirmed by soldiers erecting tents in the streets and yards.

Worse still were the burned and broken bodies lying where they'd fallen. He didn't see any Naerans among them, only invaders, leading him to conclude the legionnaires tended to their brethren first before bothering with the enemy dead.

What purpose is served by all this death and destruction?

A mixture of pity, anger, and even hate stirred in his breast as he realized the number of dead and wounded far exceeded what he saw here, and he prayed for serenity to control the unfamiliar emotions rising in him.

At last, his escort brought him to Raldus who sat on the steps of what remained of the fort commander's residence holding his red-plumed helmet in both hands as he watched the work with glazed eyes within dark circles.

There was a time where the monk would have used a teasing remark to both lighten the mood and humble the warrior, but he knew that this was the time for compassion alone.

"How are you, my friend?" he sighed as he sat down next to his protégé.

"I'm alive," Raldus responded, his voice sounding far away.

"That much is true of your body, but what of your spirit?" Keid challenged, meeting the young man's green eyes with a soft, but unyielding, smile when he turned toward him.

The warrior chuckled as he caught onto the priest's full meaning, then sighed as he returned his gaze to the men clearing the roads and stabilizing the buildings.

"I chose to destroy the works of our own hands rather than let them fall to the enemy. Many on both sides died so the rest can keep fighting. How am I supposed to feel about all of this?"

"What *are* you feeling?"

"Tired. Numb."

"That sounds right to me."

"No sadness. No sense of victory. No anger or hate. How is that right?"

The monk sighed as he leaned back and looked up to the sky for inspiration, expecting to spot the first stars coming out but instead discovering they were veiled behind the lingering smoke.

How was an old man who'd never known war supposed to offer advice and comfort to one so young who'd trained for battle his entire life?

"One does not have time to feel in the midst of a storm, and only has enough strength to pick up the pieces after it passes. When that task is done, the only consideration for body and mind is rest. Only when that is accomplished is there room for one to process his thoughts and emotions," he explained, thinking back to the thunderstorms that ravaged his own home far too often.

His friend's eyes peered into nothingness as he pondered these words until at last he sighed and rose to his feet.

"I suppose you're right. I should get back to work."

"That's not what I said. Now is the time for you to rest so you are ready for what tomorrow brings."

"I'm not going to bathe and sleep while others who are just as tired keep working," Raldus insisted, the fire returning to his voice.

"No one is as tired as a man who both leads and works. You must rest," Keid urged, punctuating his point by standing and looking up into the taller man's eyes.

Raldus glared at him for but a moment, then looked away and nodded, proving his fatigue by giving up so quickly.

"Come with me back to the city. Share what you can of your burden with me, then take your ease. People can do without you for a few hours."

The warrior nodded again, and the two of them walked off together back to the relative safety and order of Izagion.

The latest news from the front was much the same as all the rest the last two weeks, leading Triume Vejalon to do nothing but skim the paper report before handing it back to the messenger and dismissing him with a nod.

It seemed victory was within their grasp when the surviving Naeran legions retreated to a single city and fort at the furthest edge of their territory, but now the siege dragged on with no end in sight. No end except for the lives of hundreds of their citizens who believed the triumvirate, whom they revered almost as if they were gods, would lead them to a new age of prosperity in the outside world.

So far, they'd found little more than death and destruction.

Sighing, the triume wandered out to the temple balcony, clasping his hands inside their sleeves as he stood looking over the city. It seemed this was all he did these days, and each time he came out here, the sprawling metropolis below him felt ever more subdued, as if dying little by little.

For most of the war to date, Vejalon had walked among the people two or three times a week, assuring them that all was under control despite so much going to the army that those left behind barely had enough to live day-to-day. He insisted the war would be over soon, and when it was, the comforts they knew before would return, along with luxuries beyond imagining.

Or so he told them, but as this latest siege dragged on, he found he could not continue preaching what he now knew in his own heart to be a lie. This was especially true when he had to look into the eyes of those mothers, fathers, wives, and children who had lost sons, husbands, and fathers in a conflict spiraling out of control.

If only Jasud hadn't lost all sense of reason and honored the traditions which had guided them for so long, there would still be hope. Alas, he no longer recognized the votes of his fellow triumes and now commanded the army as if he were their people's sole leader.

So here he remained, sitting or standing in the temple above the great crystal towering over their great city, awaiting word that he feared would never come.

Even worse was another question growing in his mind. An unthinkable possibility that nevertheless could no longer be ignored, and for which they were ill-prepared.

What if they not only lost this war, but the enemy came here to destroy them?

What if these were the last days of a civilization which had endured for over two millennia?

A sudden gust billowed out his robes behind him, and he shuddered from a chill brought not by the wind, but from the darkness hollowing out his insides and threatening to swallow him whole.

Oh, that he had never lived to see such days.

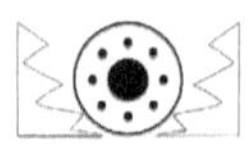

"Remember, no noise," Mettius whispered. The flickering orange light of a campfire shone over the grass beneath which they now crouched, but it was yet dim enough to ensure the approaching warriors were out of earshot of any potential sentries.

He looked full in the face of each of the ten men with him and received a confident nod from the Stoneforge Warriors and senate consularians. For this mission, they'd left behind the armor looted from the enemy for the greater mobility and stealth afforded by their own leather ensembles, bringing with them only the advanced swords which they already held in their hands.

When he was sure all knew the importance of their task, he nodded sharply, drew his sword, and turned back to face his objective when the others snuck off through the grass in either direction.

He took one step every two seconds, listening as he went, the blades of grass parting from his passage then soundlessly falling back into place. Timing was everything if they were to do this right, and he must arrive at the invader's outpost the same time as the other group whose expected progress he tracked in his mind.

If only they could disable the enemy siege weapons in this manner, but alas, scout reports revealed those machines to be protected by dozens of soldiers and the emplacements well-lit by their flameless torches.

The grass thinned, smoke tickled his nostrils, and light flickered across his face, bringing him to a halt to avoid revealing himself.

Through the mix of thin stalks topped with seeds and drooping leaves, he spotted an enemy soldier standing guard with his back to a small bonfire, appearing as a polished statue in the light of the overly large blaze.

He knelt in the dirt, using the opportunity to relieve the soreness in his legs, the muscles of which were screaming at him for walking so far at a crouch.

When the figures on the map in his mind were seconds from their final positions, he rose again, tensing every muscle in his body as he coiled to strike.

Then he burst from his position with sword raised high, setting upon the sentry who only had time to let out a surprised grunt before one of his people's own swords was thrust into his gut.

Mettius grabbed the man's spear with his free hand before it could clatter to the ground, withdrawing his blade at the same time and taking hold of the rim of the man's chestplate with that hand. He gently lowered the soldier to the ground, all the while watching his eyes for any sign of resistance, then crouched over him until the light went out from those yellowish irises.

When it was safe, he placed the spear back in the man's hand and set it against his chest, then wiped his sword on the grass before rising and strolling up to the fire, its heat drawing forth more sweat on this warm, humid night. He was soon joined by the others who each nodded to indicate the deed was done, and he looked around to see only darkness filled with the sounds of birds and the occasional scream of a fox.

"We were never here."

"What is Jasud doing about this?" Yalina demanded to know as she gazed upon the twelve bodies lined up on the ground between her and the still smoldering ashes of a watchfire.

"Nothing. He refuses to even let anyone tell him about these attacks now. He's completely obsessed with winning this battle," Avlana explained.

"How are the soldiers?"

"Not well. Their loyalty remains unquestionable, but many of them expect to die in the coming days. They aren't sleeping, with those here having all been on watch at the same time, and they fight with less vigor in each assault."

The triume hid her hands in her robes and strode down the line of bodies, all of them still wearing armor with arms lying at their sides, then back to her best agent who watched her expectantly with tired eyes.

"Perhaps they are no longer eager to indulge Jasud's obsession and are ready to listen once again to the true will of the triumvirate. Find out how many are willing to stand down by my order, even if he should object," she declared. Avlana bowed swiftly, then hurried off to the main encampment.

Was it possible this situation could be salvaged after all?

"Now! Do it now!"

The order fell on deaf ears as the trumpeter froze, tightly gripping his instrument at his right side as he stared wide-eyed at a blood-drenched enemy soldier charging straight at him with a spear raised in the air.

Raldus pounced between the two, rammed his shield into the invader's face to send him flying to the ground, then stepped forward and finished him off by slashing the tip of his sword across the man's throat.

He whirled around to face the signalman, and advanced on him until he was so close to the man's pale face that he was forced to look into his champion's eyes.

"Send. The. Signal," Raldus breathed, his rough tone not without an element of compassion.

This broke the hold of fear on the man who set his jaw as he nodded understanding, then he stepped back and raised the brass trumpet to his lips.

As the sharp call rang in his ears, Raldus returned his gaze to the field of battle between Izagion and Fort Aquasvigilate. He'd pulled most of the soldiers defending that stretch of line down to the lake during the night, discreetly out of the enemy's sightline.

That morning, the invaders took the bait and sent their latest assault against those who remained clustered around the river bridge in the hopes of severing the support line between the two fortifications as they continued to rain fire down on both the fort and city. They broke through the first defensive line with its trenches and wooden spikes within the first hour, pushing the defenders into a tight group around the bridge. Some were even forced to stand in the water to grant space for as many as possible to gain relative safety under the arrows loosed from the archers posted on the bridge itself.

Many legionnaires had broken from the fighting completely, running to safety at either the fort or city within full sight of the attackers.

Unlike at Nelius, this time it was all part of the plan.

Now that the invaders were committed and confident of their first success in weeks, it was time to finish this.

The blaring trumpet call reverberated around the field, piercing through all other noise and causing many on both sides to hesitate upon registering the sound.

Before the single, long note fully faded away, another answered from behind the Naeran lines, followed by the roaring battlecry of hundreds of men.

Those in the field took up the cry, raising their swords high and howling at the top of their lungs as their adversaries slowly backed away, disturbed by this sudden turn in the mood of the defenders.

Then a rolling thunder rose from the direction of the lake, and all perceived the eyes of the blue-armored attackers grow larger above their masks as their gaze turned to the rear of the Naeran formation.

"THIS ENDS TODAY!" Raldus shouted over the rising roar of thousands of feet striking the ground, raising his sword high for all to see and pointing it at the enemy.

His legionnaires responded with another triumphant shout as their reinforcements came into view, thousands of footsoldiers flanked by hundreds of horsemen among whom was his own father, no doubt at the head of his section.

At this sight, the enemy soldiers turned and fled as the supposedly scattered defenders charged after them, the newcomers hot on their heels.

Any pain or fatigue within Raldus evaporated as he led that charge with the sun shining upon them from above to illuminate this change in their fate.

"Hold the line!" Bujon commanded his men upon seeing many of them falter at the sight of their comrades running back at them.

His admonition did little good as many of the men on the camp's defensive line kept looking side to side at their comrades or over their shoulders in search of an escape route instead of focusing on the savage horde rushing toward them on foot and horse.

The zishna stepped up behind his men and raised his staff high, but found he could not use the weapon without too high a risk of striking his own soldiers fleeing before the screaming barbarians. He looked around for a high place from which he could fire over the heads of his people, but there was nothing.

He had just enough time to wonder why they never built fortifications for their camps like those of their enemy before the battle was joined.

"Let us through!"

"Help!"

"Move aside!"

The arriving soldiers begged for passage through the line, but the enemy was too close to risk opening gaps in their defense.

"Turn and fight!" Bujon berated, but it was too late.

The savages were upon them!

Those in the back screamed as they were cut down, inciting greater fervor upon those at the front who started pulling their comrades out of the line and pushing past them in a desperate attempt to find safety.

"Stop this! You are Zaqulons, not savages! Stand and fight!"

The words were scarcely out of his mouth before the line broke and all started to run from the fury unleashed upon them. Bujon tried to grab those nearest him and shove them back toward the enemy, but they pushed him down and kept going.

He jumped up only for another soldier to collide with him and tumble to the ground, hastily scrambling to his feet before resuming his escape.

With none of his soldiers standing their ground and the enemy only a few paces away, Bujon had no choice but to follow them.

"Cowards! Get back there! *Fight*!" Triume Jasud screamed at the soldiers streaming past the command tent.

No reaction.

"Augh!"

He raised his staff toward them, but a pair of strong hands grabbed his arm and pulled it down, forcing him to stumble to avoid being yanked to the ground.

The pressure released, and he whirled around with teeth bared to confront who would dare touch a god, barely restraining himself when he recognized Yalina's top agent with the triume herself right behind her.

"You will not harm our own people," Yalina exhorted as her amber eyes bore into his own.

"They must fight!"

"We've lost. All that remains now is to return home."

"We *cannot* lose!" Jasud bellowed.

Spinning around and raising his staff in the same motion, he fired a stream of light at the approaching primitives, narrowly missing his own agent who ducked under the reddish light as he approached.

"Report," Yalina demanded when no one else spoke.

"I fear that the battle is lost, Honored Triumes. We must retreat and gather our forces to defend our gains," Bujon confessed.

"No! I'll deal with this myself!" Jasud declared as he stepped forward.

"We cannot allow you to die here. Agents, restrain him and follow me," Yalina argued. Avlana instantly moved to obey, but Bujon stood there looking from each person to the next then back at the rapidly approaching Naerans.

"You dare?!" Jasud accused, raising his staff to burn down the two traitors, but Bujon grabbed the arm before he could fire at the same time Avlana seized hold of the other one.

"*Release me! Cowards and traitors! You will all burn!*"

Hysteric screeching broke through the noise of battle, drawing Raldus' attention to a hill atop which he beheld four people beside an elaborate white tent. Two of them held a third kicking and screaming over their heads, hustling away from the battle while the fourth knelt and retrieved one of their staff weapons from the ground. Although he was still too far away to get a clear look, Raldus marked this one to be an old woman due to her long white hair flowing over voluptuous blue robes with sparkling white trim.

Was this woman a leader of these mysterious people?

The bearded old man in similar robes but borne aloft by the armored soldiers, one of which wore a helmet with a white plume, screeched a phrase which Raldus did not understand, but his bearers paid him no heed as they took him into the mass of fleeing soldiers.

As he watched, Raldus met the old woman's gaze as she took one last look at the scene before her, and he raised his shield in anticipation of her using that staff on him. Yet, all she did was give him a look full of sadness before turning and following after the others.

"Champion?" a prime questioned upon approaching Raldus as he stood passive amidst the chaos.

"Send a runner to signal the fleet to send any ships it can downriver to harass the enemy. The cavalry shall also pursue the invaders as long as they are able before returning here. The invaders must not be allowed to regroup. Call back the infantry."

"Shouldn't we all pursue until the enemy is utterly destroyed?"

"No. Victory is ours. I will not risk that being taken away from us in an ambush; the men are tired, and there is much work to be done here. Call them back," Raldus insisted.

The officer acknowledged the order with a nod, and the trumpeter sounded the recall signal of three notes in quick succession.

Trusting his men to begin the cleanup, Raldus trudged up the hill to that tent in the hope of finally learning who it was they faced and possibly even why.

Chapter Nineteen

Aftermath

As Legate Tullus and Eagle Legion neared Naera, the first to return following the siege of Izagion, the men became more and more silent until none dared even a simple whisper. Tullus knew it was because the same dread gripping his own heart also grew within the soldiers with every step they took toward their beloved capital.

Would they be struck down with unrelenting tears when the metropolis straddling the river came into view? What evils had the invaders wrought upon their beautiful city during their short stay? Did any of it yet stand?

This despair lodged itself in his throat and expanded with each burned house, inn, and field they passed until he was sure he would black and fall off his black destrier.

All seemed in order when the gleaming white city first came into view, but he dared not hope until he knew for sure the magnificent buildings erected over many generations still stood proud and strong.

When at last he entered through the northern gate at the head of his personal guard, he finally let out all these emotions with a long sigh of relief as they dismounted.

"Ready yourselves. They may yet be waiting to exact a last revenge," he ordered the twenty-eight legionnaires with him, his voice scarcely more than a whisper. Steel hissed on wood as they drew their swords, the sound unnaturally loud in the deserted gate plaza, then they proceeded into the city proper.

Little more than garbage blew about the cobblestones as he led his soldiers past the villas of the upper class, around the consul's residence, and toward the central plaza. Every sound instantly drew the gaze of those nearest to it, and all peered into every shadow around the gates and compound walls, but nothing came forth to threaten them.

The melody of rushing water greeted the legionnaires after many agonizingly long minutes, echoing down the empty streets to lure them to the place of their nation's birth.

They reached the stairs to the river platform without any trouble and climbed them to the plaza with its shrines and forums which they found just as abandoned as the rest of the city.

"Keslu have mercy," a soldier whispered. Many echoed the sentiment upon looking at the center where the bronze statue of Keslu lay on the ground amid stones from the waist-high wall where it was crushed by its fall. The globe once held aloft by the sky god's mighty arms had broken free and rolled to the edge of the platform where it now lay past the debris of two stone shrines obliterated by its passage.

There was a time when Tullus would have been greatly disturbed by this, but now he merely noted an oddity in how little he cared to see an object of his people's worship defiled.

"Runner, return to the legion. Tell them to enter the city and search it for any stragglers. The rest of you, set up a perimeter here," the legate ordered, relaxing his posture and sheathing his sword as he spoke.

Each of the twenty-eight hustled away to carry out his orders with the efficiency he'd come to expect while he strolled to the east stairs and gazed at the colonnaded senate building.

So—their people were going to live on after all.

"Go and live well in the peace brought to you by your champion and brave legionnaires," Raldus declared to the family unit gathered around its wagon at the crossroads.

"The name Raldus Velix Praelior will be remembered for all time!" the burly patriarch announced as he gave the champion and his retinue a wide wave, stretching his arm upward as far as it would go.

Raldus returned the wave with a wide grin, then clicked his tongue as he spurred his horse, resuming the column's journey back to the capital.

He was soon leaning back on his white stallion, feeling light enough to float off even while wearing his armor, smiling under his red-plumed helmet as he looked down the road at the land he'd saved once again.

"If that head of yours gets any bigger, it's going to drag you off your horse," an irritating voice from his right shattered his glorious daydream.

He looked over at Keid, almost appearing as one with his gray mare due to his similarly colored robes, who gazed back at him with one eyebrow raised and teasing laughter in his brown eyes.

All that Raldus experienced over the past year and a half came flooding back to him as he looked into those eyes, from nearly dying at the hands of vagabond bandits to learning about Rosjen and finally to the horrors endured at Izagion. When he looked away, the weight of these memories and the feelings that came with them escaped in a long exhalation as he leaned over his horse's white mane and set his eyes on the road.

"Is this why I let you come with me? To ruin my good mood?" he joked.

"That's not the only reason. I'm well-practiced in ruining bad moods as well."

The two of them shared a light laugh which served to dispel both the arrogance that was swelling within Raldus and the grief caused by Keid's admonition. Afterward, the warrior noticed his helmet seemed unusually heavy, so he released the reins to reach up and undo the leather strap at his chin while he used his knees to keep the horse from straying.

Unwilling to halt the entire column to give him time to tie the helmet to the back of his horse, he tucked it against his gut and held it with his right hand as he took up the reins again in his left.

"That's better," Keid encouraged with a warm smile, much like the one Raldus now bore as he continued to look ahead.

It certainly did feel a lot better to have the cool breeze blowing through his hair, drying the sweat on his face and neck. The heat and humidity of summer yet persisted under the overcast autumn sky, but the wind still managed to bear with it the promise of more refreshing days soon to come.

This new pleasantness did not last long. The steady beat of a galloping horse pounding against the stone bricks rose up behind them, causing him to perk up in his saddle and peer over his shoulder in anticipation of what new trouble was coming their way.

"Champion!" the rider called out.

Raldus pulled back on his reins as the officer of his guards called a halt for the column. The young man in red tunic with a sword dangling from the belt at his waist quickly caught up to him, his brown mare rearing back at the sudden stop, then stood there snorting as its rider handed over a leather pouch.

"A message for you, Champion."

"Is there trouble?"

"No, not to my knowledge. It's from your home," the messenger explained, casting a wary glance at Keid who now sidled closer to see the news for himself. This brought him within Raldus' reach who seized the opportunity to pass his helmet over for the monk to hold. Only then did he accept the pouch, holding it with one hand and opening it with the other while once again using his knees to keep his charger from getting any ideas.

The flawless calligraphy he recognized as being written by Abbot Jerald himself, which was probably the grumpy old man's way of showing he cared. A great warmth spread throughout Raldus and his heart fluttered as he read the news. It was all he could do to resist shedding a tear in the presence of the soldiers.

When he was sure he could speak without his voice breaking, he announced the news to Keid.

"Ariela has given birth to a daughter. Both she and the baby are strong and healthy."

"Glory be to Rosjen!" Keid cried out.

Raldus read the letter again, relishing the happy news, then tucked the parchment under the collar of his tunic beneath the shining steel breastplate.

"Rest your horse and ride with us for a time. I have a reply for you to take back," he told the messenger as he handed back the pouch. He then reached for his helmet, which Keid returned without remark but with a curious expression on his face.

Before Raldus could order the prime to resume the march, Keid trotted up to the officer, signaled him to lean over with a wave, then whispered into his ear.

What was this troublemaking monk up to now?

When Keid finished, the prime grinned at Raldus, then spurred his brown warhorse ahead of the column before stopping in the center of the road and turning back toward the men watching him with confused anticipation. Then he stood in his stirrups and shouted for all to hear.

"Our champion is now a father!"

All the men cheered as they banged on their shields, celebrating not only the good fortune of one who had earned their admiration, but also the coming of new life after having faced so much death.

As Raldus watched, unsure of what to do, the voices of men and pounding of fists on wood melded into one sound which reverberated through the trees on either side and sent flocks of birds darting into the sky.

When it faded and the serene sounds of nature began to return, Keid pulled up close to Raldus to conclude his earlier teaching.

"Some things are worth celebrating."

"Have you ever heard the city so quiet?" Vejalon breathed, his breath fogging in the pre-dawn air, disappearing into the red glow from the great crystal beneath. Already the days grew colder in this mountain crater they called home, but that chill was nothing compared to the one freezing the souls of the Zaqulon people.

"No," Yalina whispered, her voice nearly inaudible in the stillness of the temple balcony.

"It is as if the foundations themselves bear the loss of every life wasted in this war. Even the light of Zaqu-ishna dims."

"The great crystal's light has been fading for decades."

"Do you think they know this is the end?" Vejalon speculated as he leaned over the balcony wall to peer into the city below where only a few lights burned in the darkness of the early hour.

"You forget yourself. Nothing is ended yet," Yalina chastised.

"There is no future remaining for us. Zaqu-ishna and all its children will die, and we will soon follow."

"That will not happen for many years, even decades. Our people have faced hardship before and always found a way through."

"This war expended all our strength, *their* strength. What else is there to do?"

The older woman moved up beside the triumvirate's junior member and placed a hand on his back as she leaned over to look into his face to deliver her next statement.

"It is up to us to find a way, and so long as I live, I will not stop looking for it."

He met her eyes and took heart in the depths of wisdom he saw within. Sighing, he stood straight again and turned to walk inside with her keeping pace next to him.

"What does Jasud have to say about our next step?" he asked once they'd settled into their cushioned chairs, glancing at the empty seat as he did so.

"He refuses to speak to anyone or come out of his private chambers. The responsibility for finding a new course falls to us alone," Yalina scoffed.

"It always should have," Vejalon mused. His fellow triume fixed him with a critical gaze, and he recoiled in anticipation of the coming censure for his disrespect of protocol, but she said nothing and her expression grew tired instead.

A tiredness of the soul which every Zaqulon must be experiencing in that moment.

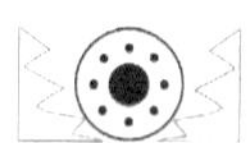

The ravine that once served as an inviting threshold between the drudgery of the world and the comforts of home for all Stoneforge Warriors now stood dark and threatening before Mettius and the seven warriors behind him. It may have felt less alien if at the least they were clad in their own leather armor, but prudence had them equipped in looted invader armor, the green paint of which now stood out against the changing colors of the forest behind the group. There hadn't been any reports, but it was possible small groups of enemy soldiers were still roaming the territory intent on causing any damage they could.

Enough of this foolishness, Mettius chided himself, then set his jaw and marched into the shadows.

None of them bothered with a torch in the dim light filtering down from high above as they were fully confident their feet knew where to step on this ancestral path, and only their footfalls echoing off the stone walls could be heard to welcome them home.

A thin light appeared ahead, and Mettius approached first to see that most of the rubble remained to block the entrance, leaving only enough room for one man to pass through at a time, same as when he was last here.

He went through with his right hand above his face, shielding his eyes from the coming brightness, scenting wood smoke and cooking meat as he passed to the other side.

"Halt! Declare yourself!" an unseen man demanded amid the sound of a blade being drawn from a wooden sheath.

Mettius turned toward the source, then dropped his hand and fixed the challenger with an irritated gaze upon recognizing the man in dirty white tunic and leather armor.

"The day I have to declare myself to you, Primus, is the day the Stoneforge Order is truly dead," he taunted.

"Master Mettius?" Primus breathed.

At a nod from the elder warrior, the sentry sheathed his sword and drew close in the same motion, his eyes darting to the next man to exit the ravine.

"My apologies. I did not recognize you in that armor. Is that not what the invaders wear?" Primus apologized as his eyes looked the elder up and down.

"Spoils of war," Mettius responded, glancing about at the rubble that used to be a town as he spoke.

The destruction was the same as when he investigated the attack with his son, but he saw no remains of human or animal, so those must have gotten buried or burned at the very least.

All the warriors accompanying him were now through the ravine, so Mettius posted one of them at the entrance before leading the rest further into the hollow.

He could now see wispy smoke rising toward the wispy clouds above before settling back to disperse within this bowl-shaped hole in the mountain. He followed this beacon to the campfire where the two soldiers assigned to Primus sat on logs, one of them turning the carcass of a deer on a spit while the other watched it cook. They jumped up when they saw the approaching warriors, but Mettius gestured for them to remain seated by flapping his hand toward the ground.

"What is the situation here?" Mettius asked of Primus as the others gathered around the fire, eager to claim a portion of venison.

"It took many weeks, but we were able to track down the origin of the invaders. Their defenses prevented us from getting too close, but we determined they come from a great city within the mountains across the cursed sea from Esbera."

"Now we know why that area is cursed," Mettius mumbled, then spoke plainly, "Anything else?"

"No. We returned here and did what we could to clean up the damage while awaiting word from the order or republic. I considered leaving many times, but without knowing how the war was going, I believed it too great a risk and feared losing the information we'd gained."

"You did the right thing, but it's safe now. The invaders have been driven out of republic lands," Mettius assured the younger warrior, then addressed his next order to the soldiers. "The two of you will set out for the capital tomorrow morning and report the location of the enemy city to the senate. You will also pass the word to any surviving Stoneforge citizens that it is time for them to return and begin rebuilding."

Both men confirmed the order with a nod, and Mettius released all of them to eat and take their ease for the evening.

As for him, he wandered off to the sacred pool by the ravine, taking a few pieces of meat on a wooden plate to the sentry as he passed by. The sun sank to the horizon as he sat there, bringing on the chill of night in that hollow place between stone cliffs, but he noticed none of this as he stared into those clear waters, meditating on all that had happened and was coming.

"Fort Nelius and Fort Merivista are both regarrisoned. All cities and towns have been reclaimed, and no invaders are to be found within our borders," Legate Tullus announced to the senate, now returned to the city and restored to its rightful place in the expansive debate chamber.

"We've received reports of Mortuns coming up from the south to raid and torment our people. What of them?" a senator demanded to know.

"Less than a hundred of them were bold enough to leave their swamps to plunder what they could following the withdrawal of the invaders. All of them are now either dead or have fled home."

"Then it is finished."

"It is too early to draw that conclusion, Senator. All I can say with any certainty at this time is that our territory is secure and the people are safe."

"What else is there?"

"We do not know the plans of the enemy, nor how badly we have hurt them. This may only be a respite as they regroup to attack again."

"Did we ever determine their identity?" the consul spoke up.

"All we have learned is a name. Zaqulon, discovered by the champion following our victory at Izagion."

"This name does not appear in any known text. It must be a new god determined to create a domain for himself," a senator chimed in.

"They inflicted considerable damage to our shrines and temples before evacuating the capital, so it certainly was an army belonging to any of *our* gods," another speculated further.

The legate bit his tongue to resist contradicting his political leaders, thinking back to the peace and calm he saw within Raldus and his monk companion during the siege, no matter how dire the situation became. As the battle dragged on, he came to believe they were deriving strength from some supernatural force of the kind he'd never seen demonstrated by the so-called gods of which the politicians now spoke.

"He must be a god of little consequence given our defeat of his army; therefore, his identity is meaningless. Let us celebrate this victory while we can!" the consul announced, eliciting a single cheer from the assembly.

"As you wish," Tullus concluded with a bow.

His business concluded, he spun around with a twirl of his blue cape and marched from the room, the thought of celebration least in his mind as he dwelled on the day's remaining duties.

Chapter Twenty

Turning of the Tide

Although annoyed that the legate's summons came during his midday meal, Raldus set a brisk pace through the ornate halls of the senate building, ignoring the snobbish looks of elites in their togas and armored consularians at his simple attire of belted tunic and sandals.

The door to the legate's office stood open, so he entered without announcing himself to find two soldiers streaked with filth standing in front of the desk behind which stood Legate Tullus himself.

"What has happened?" Raldus questioned, his voice heavy with concern.

"These two report they discovered the location of the invader's home city," Tullus explained. The warrior looked into the soldier's faces, first recognizing them as the ones he left with Primus, then seeing the truth of this in their eyes.

"Where?"

"In the mountains south of Carish Lar," one of the soldiers reported.

Raldus glanced at Tullus, in whose face he saw the same despair threatening to take hold of his own heart, then back at the soldiers.

"Is it possible to get an army through those mountains?"

"Primus believes so."

"I've already sent word to my best scouts to rendezvous with Primus and work with him to find a route," Tullus revealed and Raldus nodded his approval.

"Does the senate know?" he asked next.

"Not yet," the legate responded, then directed his next statement to the soldiers, "Clean yourselves up and get some rest. I'll summon you to give the details to a mapmaker later."

The soldiers saluted by placing their right fists over their hearts, bowed, and walked out of the room, honoring Raldus with a quick "Champion" as they passed him.

"I wanted to discuss the matter with you and settle on a course of action before we address the senate together," Tullus confessed once the soldiers were gone.

"It seems clear that we must assault this city if we are to ensure it will never threaten our people again."

"Yes, except I foresee two complications. First, the senate's attitude regarding these invaders and our victory over them concerns me. It makes me wonder if another victory will inflate their egos and turn them into tyrants with an unquenching lust for greater power."

"I've wondered the same, but they would not be where they are if they did not already lust for power. We cannot know the true nature of men's hearts or what they will become. We can only act on the information we have, which is that these Zaqulons still pose a threat to our people," Raldus deduced.

The legate accepted this truth with a nod before continuing.

"Second, our resources were greatly depleted by the invasion, made all the worse by the wars fought only a few months prior. They may not be gods, or empowered by any, but it cannot be denied this enemy possesses great power. I would hesitate to attack their home even if we were at full-strength."

"If there is one thing at which Naerans excel, it is overcoming seemingly impossible odds and coming out all the stronger for it. Send a messenger to Kostrai requesting reinforcements to bring our assault force to the strength it will need."

"We could also bring in conscripts from Esbera," Tullus mused. He looked down at the map spread out on his table as he slowly sank into his chair, placing his hands on the desktop as he dwelled on the possibilities.

"I go to don my armor, then I will return to face the senate with you," Raldus apprised, then turned and marched out of the room upon receiving an affirming nod.

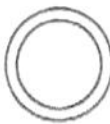

"What has brought you to us tonight, brother?" Keid asked as he stepped back from the door to give Tullus room to enter. It was common for members of his faith to address each other as brother and sister, but he usually preferred to address people by their name and only used the term now to assure the Naeran he was truly one of them following his statement of faith shortly after their return to the city.

"Politics," the legate grumbled, plodding over to the low table beside which Raldus already reclined on white cushions. He took the space to the warrior's right while Keid closed the heavy oak door before rejoining them by taking the chair across from his young friend.

"Yes, we were discussing some of that ourselves," Raldus remarked as he poured wine into a silver goblet.

"They're convinced we've defeated an army of the gods. The consul actually sees this as a chance to become a god himself," Tullus explained.

"What do you think?" Keid challenged.

"I think they're all fools, but I have to keep that to myself if I don't want to lose my head."

"You still haven't told anyone else about your conversion, have you?"

"No."

"Why?"

The legate sighed, set his goblet on the table with a loud sigh, then looked at Raldus for support.

"They will think he can no longer be trusted and remove him from his position," the warrior explained.

"Who?"

"Everyone," Tullus answered.

"Is your position more important to you than your faith?"

"He's right to stay silent for now," Raldus interjected, and Keid fixed him with a glare mixing anger and disappointment.

"You should know better."

The young man switched from lying on his shoulder to his elbow, raising himself up to fix the monk with a gaze equal in fervor.

"You are the one who does not understand the politics of a nation. Tullus is a part of our success in this war, and he is needed to finish it. His replacement could be a fool moved into the position by the senate out of spite instead of merit because of what they will see as a betrayal, and all will be lost. They may even come to distrust me and cease to heed my words."

"I've heard enough," Tullus intervened before the argument could continue, and both men turned their gazes upon him as he stared into the purple liquid within his goblet.

They waited in silence for him to gather his thoughts, held in place by the weight of the tension now filling the room.

"I do feel compelled to share what I have learned and now believe, but I'm also convinced that the time is not right. I could not forgive myself if I were forced to sit out the remainder of this war, but once it is over, I will speak up and deal with any consequences that come from my decision," he described.

The monk and warrior looked at each other, their eyes revealing that this conversation would continue another time, but for now they were satisfied with this conclusion.

"Let us rest now. Tomorrow will bring its own challenges," Keid admonished before excusing himself and heading for his room.

"So, even the great and mighty Naerans admit they need help," Neacal boasted.

Any conversation helped to alleviate the boredom if nothing else as he trudged down the road in the midst of a thousand other warriors. The days were growing colder, but he remained quite comfortable in his loose-fitting wool shirt, pants, and leather boots, and not even the weight of his armor and weapons slung over his broad shoulders bothered him.

"They would never do that. I overheard the messenger tell the chief that they were looting so much treasure the senate decided to be generous, but of course we have to go get it for ourselves," Bhatair argued, and the two shared a hearty laugh.

"Yes, I'm sure there could be no other reason for them to ask all the tribes to march to war but to carry off what they could otherwise keep for themselves," Neacal played along.

The two of them had been friends all their lives; a friendship forged hunting in the forests, carousing in the taverns, and fighting barbarians in the north. There was no one he trusted more to be at his side in these unusual times when those who had always protected them called on them for aid for the first time, at least on such a grand scale.

"Rumor is the king promised to send five-thousand."

"It'll be two or three times that if everyone goes."

"Some will stay behind to guard the homeland should we find defeat."

"Ha! Even if we lose whatever battle for which we've been summoned, no one will ever soundly defeat the Naerans and move close enough to threaten us," Neacal scoffed.

When his friend did not respond, he glanced over to see the burly, red-bearded man staring at the white bricks upon which they strode, any expression that might give away his thoughts hidden by the thick braids of red hair dangling over his shoulder.

"I'm not so sure," he finally admitted.

"No one has ever defeated the republic in war!"

"There was Izagion."

"That was more of a stalemate than a defeat."

"I've heard tales of this new enemy they face. Most say they are sent by the gods themselves. It's also been said that the gods the Naerans once served chased them out of their homeland, driving them here. Perhaps they've come to finish the job and drive them into the sea?"

"You worry too much, my friend!" Neacal bellowed, cheerfully slapping the man on the back so hard as to make him stumble.

A deep, echoing voice floated toward them from the front of the jumbled collection of men.

"Sounds like Martain is trying his hand at songwriting again," Bhatair mumbled upon not recognizing the lyrics within the familiar tune.

The words drifting back to them first spoke of their tribe migrating from the frigid north in search of more hospitable lands and finding them on the edge of an enormous forest. Next, it spoke of making a home beside those dark and mysterious woods from which their people drew provision and fear in equal measure, then of allying with the other tribes that followed to form the kingdom of Kostrai.

Finally, the singer reflected on the call to arms that put them on the march into foreign lands, speculating on what they would find at the end of the road. He prayed for all the warriors to be instilled with courage and for a swift victory in the coming battle.

The rest of the men took up the song when it became a familiar lament for hearth and home. It passed into republic lands ahead of them, reverberating through the trees and back to the warriors, settling into their very souls to remind them of the families and friends they left behind in order to keep them safe.

The Naerans thought the Kostrai people uncivilized, mocking them from their cities of stone, but they paid little heed to this ignorance. None had bigger hearts, and any who threatened them or their friends would soon quake in fear at the fury unleashed upon them.

Chapter Twenty-One

The Siege

"You've failed!"

"It will take decades for us to recover from this loss!"

"If we ever do!"

"What are you going to do about this?"

The nine members of Zaqulon's city council hurled these accusations and more from behind the stone table atop the dais several paces in front of Zishna Bujon as he stood there watching them with an unbothered smile. For him, the events which had stirred the politicians into such a fervor brought hope where before there was none, and this was unchanged by the fear of fools whose only duty it was to sit around talking all day.

However, it was of some concern that the triumes chose not to be involved thus far, especially since they went so far as to bar him from even entering their temple to speak with them and treating him only as the commander of the army and not as one of their own agents.

"Enough!" Administrator Hirn, leader of the council, called out.

He looked to his right and left, glaring at the other members until he was sure they would remain silent, then he leaned forward and fixed the zishna with rage thinly veiled behind simple confusion.

"Our city is surrounded by enemies you created when you failed your mission, yet you stand before us grinning as if hiding some great secret. Why?"

"It is good that our enemy has come to us," Bujon answered confidently.

"Why?"

"They were only able to drive us back with a combination of strong fortifications and greater numbers. Now they have come to where we are strongest. The guardians will burn their armies to ash which will leave their homeland defenseless. We will be free to seize it at our leisure."

The administrator leaned back, the fire in his eyes fading as he considered this strategy.

"We should not be so quick to underestimate these people. Such arrogance has already cost us once, except this time it means the destruction of our city if we fail," Warden Nelsid, leader of the city's security force, advised.

The rest of the council nodded in agreement while Bujon shook his head in disbelief.

"The power of the guardians, which comes from Zaqu-ishna itself, is far greater than anything in this world. There is nothing these savages can do against it," he insisted.

No one said anything as he studied their faces, most of which were still consumed by fear but he detected faint hope in three of them, including the administrator.

"If there was another to take your place, we would have already removed you from your position. As it is, you still hold the blessing of the triumvirate, and there is no one with your level of knowledge of the outside world. Are you certain our defenses will hold?" Hirn questioned.

"Without a doubt."

The administrator looked at his fellow councilmembers, received an affirming nod from all but one, then sighed and directed his attention back to the officer in his black suit uniform trimmed in white.

"I hope you are right. We are all dead if you're wrong."

"There are no walls protecting the enemy city?" Raldus double-checked the scout's report.

"None that we could see, Champion."

"They never expected an enemy to find them here," Mettius suggested, prompting Raldus and Tullus to each nod his agreement.

Their voices were little more than a whisper as they kept their gazes fixed on the massive colossus across the yawning crevasse at their feet. This statue of a man in skintight shorts rose over a hundred feet from the artificially flat ground at its base, the top of its head nearly level with the cliffs on either side of it which showed it must have been carved in place. Its feet were shoulder-length apart with arms at its sides as muscles large enough to make even the best of athletes jealous rippled all over its frame.

The most unsettling feature, beyond even its size, was the pair of glowing, narrow red eyes that seemed to study them as they did it. Indeed, the skill of the sculptors was such that even the most skeptical among them couldn't help but wonder if the thing would soon come alive to smite all who dared approach.

"What manner of people built such a thing, and why?" Angus Dubach, leader of the Kostrai army, breathed.

"To evoke awe and fear," Tullus speculated.

"We're wasting time," Mettius grumbled, prompting a sigh from Raldus as he turned his gaze aside.

"He's right," the champion agreed, then addressed his next words to the scout in his thin leather armor, "Your unit marked paths into the city?"

When the scout confirmed this, Raldus nodded to Tullus who in turn nodded to the trumpeter at his side. This man then blew a single, long note which reverberated off the stony cliffs down to the first wave of conscripts waiting below.

The combined roar of hundreds of men rose up in answer, and the officers looked down as the dark-skinned Esberans swarmed from the base of the cliff into the shadowy chasm between them and the colossus.

"Are you certain it is wise to send the Esberan conscripts first? They may choose to betray us," Raldus wondered aloud.

"We do not know what defenses the enemy may yet have at their disposal. It is better to find out using subjugated enemies than our own people or those of our true friends," Tullus responded candidly. The compliment evoked a grim smile from Angus who nodded once as he gazed upon the potentially doomed men below, his pity for them exceeding any pride or relief he was also feeling in that moment.

The width of the crevasse was small at its bottom, so with the first wave already halfway across, all fell silent to see what came next.

"What is that noise?" Angus declared as a low droning reverberated off the cliffs and steadily grew in volume. Coincidentally, Raldus noticed an odd sensation as if something were crawling over his skin and he raised his right arm to see all of the hairs standing up between the leather bracer and tunic sleeve.

"Look!" Mettius shouted, and all followed his outstretched arm and finger back to the colossus, the eyes of which now burned with great intensity.

"Pull them back!" Raldus ordered, having guessed at what was coming next, but it was too late.

Everyone clapped hands to ears as beams of red light, thick as tree trunks, shot out from the statue's eyes with a thunderous burst. The ground shook when they struck the floor of the chasm, and all watched in wide-eyed horror as those beams swept over the advancing conscripts and turned them to ash without any chance to turn and run.

Mere seconds later, the beams vanished, leaving nothing behind but scorched stone and the stench of burnt flesh.

"Pull back!" Raldus shouted. He pulled the kneeling scout to his feet and pushed him toward the camp, then made sure the others were on their way before taking a last look at the statue.

The air rippled as those shining eyes peered back at him, freezing his heart with the presence of evil and death incarnate burning within those red slits.

"Those monstrosities guard every path into the city. There is nothing we can do against such power," Tullus despaired to the others assembled under the pavilion in the center of their camp. The linen flapped against its frame as a frigid wind already bearing the chill of winter in this high place gusted through the assembled leaders, all of whom ignored it even as it nearly dislodged the maps and other parchments from beneath the weights holding them in place.

In this particular flat spot among the crags, mercifully shielded from the nearest colossus by those sharp ridges, there was only enough room for the top commanders of each army and their staffs. The rest of their troops were scattered amongst the cliffs anywhere a suitable enough place for a camp could be found, potentially leaving them vulnerable to ambushes, but there was no other choice for quartering their troops in this treacherous region.

"You say these people are not gods?" Angus questioned from where he stood beneath the outer edge of the canvas shading them. He looked ready to take his men and return home, and the legate found that he couldn't blame him as he was considering the same thing.

“I’m getting real tired of people asking that as if it makes any difference,” Mettius growled, sliding his foot off the stool upon which he was leaning and taking a step towards the Kostrai noble.

“We cannot defy the gods!”

“We can, we have, and we will,” Mettius insisted, punctuating his point by further advancing on his verbal opponent.

“Enough! I will not tolerate my allies fighting amongst themselves!” Tullus ended the dispute.

Both men were silent, but kept staring at each other, Mettius stiff with rage while Angus remained slack with despair and his face twisted in confusion.

“This is not the first time I’ve faced this power and heard hardened men of war declare that our doom has come,” Raldus spoke up, his tone quiet and thoughtful. Mettius glanced at his son leaning against a corner pole, then gave Angus one last look before striding over to the table to lean against it with both hands.

“This is far more powerful,” Tullus muttered despondently.

“Yes, but if one can be defeated, so can the other.”

“What are you talking about? You’ve seen this before and lived to tell the tale?” Angus questioned, drawn by his curiosity into stepping deeper into the pavilion.

“He did more than live through it. He defeated it and the one wielding it,” Mettius declared proudly.

“How?”

Raldus pushed off the pole with a sigh, walked over to stand on the opposite side of the table from Tullus, then stood with his hands clasped behind his back to tell his story.

Although having already been told these events by others, Tullus listened intently, eager to hear of it from the champion himself. He would have been there with him if not for having to lead the war against the Esberans taking place at the same time.

"The traitor Tallio Atroni raised an army against the republic while the legions were deployed to Esbera and the northern border. He seized the town of Pralacus Templum and built a fortress in the nearby mountains, receiving help from what we now know to be people from this city. When we cornered him in that fort, a stranger pinned us down using a less powerful version of what you saw this morning contained within his staff."

The champion paused to take a breath, his eyes veiled as he peered inside at the memory and not at those leaning in and hanging on to his every word.

"One of his first strikes destroyed a rock behind which soldiers had taken cover, and I soon realized that he would not shoot through the dust lingering in the air, even when more took shelter behind what remained. I threw smaller stones to intercept his next blast, and it dispersed upon striking them. In that way, I was able to close the distance and disarm him," Raldus concluded.

"I doubt we can toss stones large enough to stop this one," Angus sighed as he looked down at the ground in disappointment.

"It doesn't always work anyway. It seems that a certain type of stone is required, and the beam passes through all others," Mettius clarified.

"Toss stones," Tullus murmured as he stared at the map spread out on the table before him. He looked up to meet Raldus' gaze in whose smile it was revealed that he was thinking the same thing.

"What? What is it?" Angus questioned as he glanced from the legate to the champion and back again.

"You tell them," Raldus decreed, and Tullus turned to face the others with a smile.

"We get the engineers to design and build new siege weapons and destroy as many of those statues as needed to get the army through."

"I know you think rather highly of your engineers, but it's doubtful even they could create such a weapon," Angus despaired.

"Designing it would take months, if not years. It will be difficult to keep the army supplied for that length of time in these mountains, even if the enemy doesn't attack our lines," Mettius mused. His tone was more thoughtful than that of his counterpart, but even the hardened warrior was unable to keep a twinge of doubt from his words.

"We already have the design. The invaders gave it to us, and now we will use it to destroy them!" Tullus announced triumphantly. Mettius and Angus both looked up at him in confusion, which Raldus soon cleared up.

"When attacking our forts and cities, the invaders used a powerful weapon to fling burning jars far out of the range of our own catapults or ballistae. We've been studying descriptions from the survivors ever since, and many of them were captured after routing them at Izagion."

"Why am I just now hearing about this?" Angus questioned with suspicion creeping into his tone.

"Many things happen in war, and this wasn't relevant until now. What matters is that it should not take long to construct something suitable for our purposes," Tullus insisted.

"Why not use the captured weapons?"

"It takes a lot more power to fling stones than jars of oil, especially over that distance with stones large enough to destroy those statues," Mettius grumpily inferred after stepping up to the table to peer at the map.

"Anything powerful enough for that will need to be assembled in place," Raldus interjected.

"They'll see and destroy anything we come up with long before it's ready," Tullus mused.

"It won't be easy, but I believe it can be done."

Tullus met the champion's gaze, took heart from the unwavering confidence he saw there, then looked around at the others to see them similarly bolstered to varying degrees.

"Let's get it done."

The shoulder of Guardian Hequn-la, so named by the ancients when they constructed the colossi on the heights surrounding their great city, proved the perfect place for Zishna Bujon to perch and monitor the activities of the savages. After experiencing the power of the guardians, they'd made no further attempt to assault the city, but instead erected great wooden towers on the cliffs opposite them.

"Nine days since they first arrived, and twelve have passed with no attempt to attack nor decision to flee. What do they hope to gain by staying?" Agent Avlana questioned as she approached from out the door in the guardian's neck.

"This is a common tactic in their wars. They surround a city and wait in the expectation the inhabitants will grow desperate from disease and starvation until they are forced to surrender," Bujon explained.

"Such a thing will never happen with us. All of our food is grown in city warehouses by the light of Zaqu-ishna," Avlana scoffed.

"They do not know this, and their ignorance gives us the time we need to recover and prepare a new invasion."

As agents of different triumes, it was unusual for them to converse so cordially, if they did so at all, especially given their recent disagreements over how to conduct the war. Yet, even as their triumes continued to be at odds, the two of them had discovered an odd sense of camaraderie since returning to the city as there were few others who understood their experiences.

"They cannot believe those towers will protect them, no matter how much wood they drag out here from their homeland," Bujon sneered as they watched dozens of men use ropes to drag support beams up the hill before collapsing to their hands and knees.

"No, I think it more likely they are relying on us *choosing* not to destroy them," Avlana speculated.

"Why build them at all?" he questioned, attracting Avlana's blue-eyed gaze when he tensed up. It suddenly occurred to him that this work might not be as nonsensical as it seemed, a revelation supported by how their previous losses came about by underestimating these people.

"The reason must be to observe us from a place of comfort as the days and nights grow cold," she reasoned.

"Yes, that must be the cause," he agreed, relaxing his shoulders and moving his hand away from his sword while silently chiding himself for growing fearful.

"Come, let us return to the city. The triumvirate remains silent, and the people look to us for courage," Avlana suggested, and he nodded his consent before turning to follow.

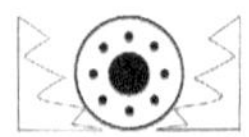

The voices and clamouring of men hard at work inside the tower hardly registered to Mettius as he stood watching the two figures atop the statue's shoulder from atop the plankway around the inside rim. He wished they were close enough for him to see their lips and discern their conversation, then half-smiled upon realizing he didn't know their language anyway.

Not long after the second person arrived, both returned to the interior of the statue, the glowing red eyes to which the old warrior had grown accustomed and no longer feared so long as their light remained steady.

So far, it seemed the Zaqulons did not know the true nature of the work taking place on the cliffs around them, nor so much as cared.

A few more days of such indifference was all the republic needed to end this—forever.

Chapter Twenty-Two

Retribution

Through the predawn sky arced a sliver of flame bearing the appearance of one last shooting star amid the fading lights of its brethren.

At the top of a tower precariously perched upon a cliff, his nostrils full of the scent of freshly cut wood, Legate Tullus saluted with fist to chest as the flaming arrow fell back to the ground.

It was time.

His armor clattered as he raced down the steps spiraling around the tower's interior while holding his sword by the hilt to keep it from swinging in its sheath. The stairs, which were merely thick tree branches anchored into the wall and braced from below by more of the same, shook as if ready to collapse with every step, but that was to be expected given their temporary nature and he spared no time worrying about it.

"Now!" he shouted to the soldiers standing at three of the corners as he drew his sword and ran to the fourth.

They struck at the ropes above the stakes to which they were tied, severing them with a single cut. The thick cords hissed as they sped through the pulleys and all four walls groaned as they tilted away.

Slow at first, then quickly as their weight took hold, the walls fell outward, crashing to the ground and kicking up dust and wind which billowed the legate's light blue cape out behind him. The wall nearest the cliff edge slid away from them and into the crevasse. Seconds later, the sounds of cracking and splintering wood echoed back up to them after it smashed on the hard ground below.

"Launch!" Tullus ordered, pointing his sword at the nearest colossus behind which the sky was starting to lighten.

The soldiers gathered around the now exposed device of gears and pulleys arrayed on a wooden frame to hold down a round length of wood long enough to serve as the mast of a ship.

To their left, another such device released its load with a deafening snap, and Tullus watched with the others as the boulder sailed through the air and past its target.

"Move!" the legate demanded when the statue's menacing red eyes started glowing brighter in the darkness as that unnatural hum once again filled the air and the hairs on the back of his neck stood up.

All three soldiers rushed over to the crank and together pulled on the pin holding it in place, grunting from the strain.

It popped free, sending the soldiers to the ground on their backsides as the throwing arm snapped up, the wind created by its passage nearly picking up the legate and tossing him into the fissure.

The boulder flew high as a crack of thunder sounded from across the chasm, and Tullus looked over in time to see two red beams aimed at them pass beneath the projectile.

Then the beams struck the siege catapult, sending all those with it flying in every direction as shrapnel pinged off their armor and shredded any exposed skin.

Legate Tullus crashed to the ground several paces away where he covered his head with both hands and screamed as extraordinary heat washed over him, but then it disappeared and was replaced by a sudden, deep silence.

Everything hurt, and blood dripped from his face onto the stony ground, but he grit his teeth and rose up enough to look across the chasm.

He smiled upon seeing the now headless colossus, then collapsed again, hearing nothing but his own labored breathing as he closed his eyes.

Shouts and distant thunder woke Zishna Bujon with a start which sent him leaping from his bed, running down the stairs, and out into the barracks courtyard in nothing but his shorts. He grabbed the nearest soldier by both shoulders, little more than a boy recruited after their return, and turned him around to shout in his face.

"What is all this noise about?"

"The guardians are falling!"

Shocked, the zishna softened his grip and the boy wriggled free to leave him standing there, his hands suspended in midair as he gawked at the western perimeter where the sky glowed orange from one or more large fires.

He recovered his senses with a quick shake of the head, then frantically glanced around the courtyard until he spotted a uniformed officer by the rank of Nharin staring into the distance.

"You!" Bujon declared, his sharp tone snapping the man from his trance and drawing his gaze. "Get these men organized and repel the attackers!"

The nharin nodded and began shouting commands as he pushed several armored soldiers into a group and ordered them to the perimeter while any without armor or weapons he sent to get equipped.

Satisfied, Bujon darted back inside his quarters to don his armor, sword, and grab hold of his beam staff.

"The way is clear! Let's go!" Raldus declared as the statue crumbled to pieces on the cliff high above him. Drawing his sword, he pointed it at the path meandering up the cliffside and gave a mighty shout as the trumpeter to his left blew a single note.

For this battle, Raldus was once again equipped in his armor from the monastery to boost his own morale with the weight of that steel serving as a constant reminder of God and home. The set of repurposed enemy gear he was previously using he'd gifted to one of the four Stoneforge Warriors who had returned from other jobs in time to be present for this final battle.

The warriors and legionnaires with him took up the shout as they raised their swords and spears in the air, then charged forward with their champion as he ran onto the path.

They encountered no resistance on the long climb up the path winding back and forth between jagged rocks, none but the steep and narrow slope which slowed even the best of them.

His legs burned, and lungs felt ready to burst, but Raldus pushed through with his men close behind. Upon reaching the top at last, they burst into the dawn's light and immediately formed a shield wall, the fog generated from their panting gasps spreading out in front of them.

Those in the front lay the flat of their blades on the top edge of their shields while those behind raised their javelins over their shoulders, and all of them squinted in the sudden brightness for any sign of movement.

Perhaps attacking east at dawn wasn't the best idea after all.

It proved to be no issue, as they still did not encounter any defenders, giving their eyes time to adjust to reveal a flat space leveled by human hands amidst the pointy crags.

"Spread out. Keep alert," Raldus whispered.

The group split apart and slowly made its way across the flat clifftop, weaving between the broken pieces of statue now littering the otherwise smooth surface. Meanwhile, legionnaires continued arriving three or four at a time behind them and formed into defensive lines to secure the rear.

A massive crater opened up before them, the edges of which were lined with dark buildings of various shapes and sizes. As they drew closer, the unnatural glow upon these structures grew stronger in the depths yet untouched by the rising sun.

"Is this a dream?"

"Such wonders exist in the mortal world?"

The warriors breathed in awe at the sight now before them, and all who beheld it dropped their guard, including Raldus.

At the center of the great city, taller than any building within and reaching a little over halfway to the top, sat an immense crystal which glowed a dark red. A lattice stretched between three pylons surrounded this phenomenon, and above it resided an ornate temple held aloft by those same pillars.

Myriad shouts drew Raldus' attention to the path below him where he spotted dozens of blue-armored soldiers rushing up at them.

"First line!" he shouted, raising his shield and stepping back in unison with his warriors.

Ten legionnaires stepped up behind those standing at the edge and lobbed their spears at the enemy. One struck a soldier in his unprotected face, killing him instantly, while the rest merely bounced off the armor, but the impact alone was enough to knock each target off-balance to send many of them rolling back down the slope.

"Second line!"

There was enough time for ten more legionnaires to switch places with the first group and throw their spears with much the same result, then the defenders were upon them.

“Come together!” Raldus ordered. The legionnaires pulled together into two circles and the warriors formed a third, those on the outside of each interlocking their shields with swords poised to strike above them while those on the inside watched the enemy and directed the others.

“Die, Savages!” a defender snarled as he rushed towards the Stoneforge circle with sword raised high. A sword to the throat made the death his, the looted weapon slicing through the mail with little trouble.

Another brazen defender ran straight for the warriors, but right before entering the reach of their arms, he jumped over them, past the men who stepped aside to avoid being knocked down, and landed in a crouch with a single hand and knew on the ground. Raldus kicked him in the face which knocked him onto his back, then finished him off by driving his sword into the man’s heart.

When he looked back at the rest of the fight, he saw their phalanxes unbroken with only a few enemies remaining.

“Break and finish them!”

The warriors and legionnaires leapt out of their formations, surrounded the half-dozen defenders, and swiftly ended their lives with swords and spears.

“Is that all?” a warrior questioned.

When he looked around, Raldus confirmed that none of his people were injured, and only the bodies of defenders littered the ground among the rubble of what now appeared to be their only real defense.

“Move out,” he grumbled, then set out for the path down.

“Yahhh!” Neacal cried out as he lifted an enemy by the throat with one hand before throwing him into a stone wall. The small man groaned as he slid to his butt on the stone pavers, then was silent and sat there unmoving.

He spun around with both hands on his greatsword, scanning the area for his next target, but there was only Bhatair standing there looking at the limp-limbed wretch by the wall.

"I expected more of a challenge. These people hardly inspire the fear of gods as told by the Naerans," his friend commented.

When he was sure there was no one else to fight, at least for the moment, Neacal lowered his blade and glanced around at their countrymen smashing through doors and looting homes among the screams of men, women, and children.

"What does it matter? Let's get our share!" he declared, heartily clapping his friend's shoulder and laughing at the mischievous grin that replaced his confusion.

"Right behind you!"

"Hold! Fight for your city!" Zishna Bujon rallied nearby soldiers. All who heard him gathered around and formed into a line, encouraging many others who were running away to do the same.

It wasn't as if there was any refuge left to which they could flee anyway, but such a fact did little to ease the rising panic to which even the zishna was not immune. However, they could still draw courage from each other as they held the line against the savage horde running amok in their home streets.

Bujon raised his staff over the heads of his kneeling men, some of whom now bore shields taken from the attackers, and fired a blast at the Naerans charging down the street toward them. Many of them were cut down by the reddish beam of light, but it did little to slow the rest who hopped over or went around their fallen comrades, eyes flashing with hate and anger within the shadows cast by their helmets.

"All of you will burn!" Bujon declared as he squeezed the trigger again, but nothing happened.

He lowered the staff and peered into the diamond-shaped glass at its head, grinding his teeth together when he saw the crystal within as dark and lifeless as any common stone.

He threw the useless gold stick at the savages, striking one of them in the head only for it to bounce off his helmet, then drew his sword.

The attackers crashed into the line, knocking all to the ground with only two of their own getting struck. Two came straight for Bujon who snarled as he lunged at them.

He blocked one strike with an armored forearm while driving his sword into the other's gut, then followed through with a punch to the first man's face. This gave him the time he needed to pull out his sword, which he slashed across his opponent's chest in the same motion.

Even the primitive steel breastplate protected against such a blow and the savage came back at him, wildly swinging his sword between them.

"Augh!" Bujon cried out at a sudden bruising pain in his right side above the hip. He turned to see a Naeran tossing aside a splintered spear shaft before reaching for his sword, but Bujon swung his own blade around and sliced off the man's hand before he could grasp the hilt.

Then he was struck on the back of the head hard enough to send him stumbling forward. He recovered quickly and spun around to find that he now faced five savages and none of his own men were to be seen.

"So be it," he declared.

He charged into them, sword at his side aimed for a thrust, but he did not get the chance to strike.

The last thing he saw was the point of a blade coming straight for his eyes.

"All is lost," Triume Jasud lamented, his voice a whisper.

He'd watched the battle from the window in his room, ignoring the agents pounding at his door, demanding he let them take him to safety. As if such a place existed for him now.

It was too late for that.

It was too late for them all.

He raised the goblet in his right hand to his lips, tilted it back to drain the last of the red liquid within, then tossed it to the floor behind him, the metal repeatedly clanging on the polished stone as a few remaining drops splashed out.

Nothing left now.

No future.

It all belonged to the savages now.

He reached up, pushed the hook holding the panes closed at the center out of its loop and pulled them into the room. This admitted the cacophony of shouts and screams below him, accompanied by almost no sound of metal on metal to show any of his people fought on.

He climbed up onto the sill, the wind at this height billowing his blue robes, grey beard, and unbraided hair out behind him as he looked down at the ground far below.

There is one victory I can yet deny them.

He smiled at the thought, even as he shivered from the cold borne by the wind seeping into his bones.

Lifting his eyes to the horizon, he closed them, took a deep breath, then dove off. This turned him toward the great crystal, and he smiled as Zaqu-ishna's light shone through his eyelids to fill him with peace in his last moments.

The attackers drew ever closer to the city center as Yalina and Vejalon watched from the temple balcony. Not even the red beams cutting through the savages slowed them down as they swept through the streets in far greater numbers than any Zaqulon had thought possible.

Fires burned across the city, the smoke of which darkened the sky on what should have been a beautiful day, and word had come that Zishna Bujon was dead after fighting to the bitter end.

Below them, the last of the Triumvirate agents were gathered at each of the three pylons, protecting the elevators accessing the temple under Avlana's command.

"We are doomed," Vejalon despaired.

Although this was true, Yalina tensed up at the breach of discipline and turned only her head to glare at the sad figure beside her.

"Our fate will be met with dignity," she chided.

He met her gaze, his dark-green eyes welling up with tears.

"All things come to an end. Let us meet ours with the pride of our people still strong in our hearts," she added in a gentler tone.

The sounds of death and destruction grew louder as they stood there looking into each other's souls, and time itself seemed to slow as the fire returned to Vejalon's eyes.

The younger triume squared his shoulders, nodded his agreement, and the two of them returned their attention to the city.

One way or another, the end of Zaqulon was near as the light of Zaqu-ishna and its children faded. There was some small comfort in knowing they'd done all that was possible to save their civilization.

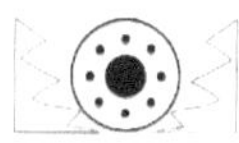

Soldiers of Naera, Kostrai, and Esbera rushed past Mettius and his warriors striding away from the fighting. Many collided with the stalwart men only to be pushed aside, and others questioned where they were going only to be ignored.

They found Raldus in the center of a plaza with the rest of the warriors, one of whom was laid out on his shield at their feet while the rest stood watching the frenzy around them. None held a weapon; all had his shield resting against his legs, and most had cuts in their looted armor through which could be seen smears of blood.

"Where is Legate Tullus? Why does he not stop this madness?" Mettius demanded as he stomped up to his son.

"Dead," Raldus responded wearily.

"So you let these men run wild, slaughtering all they find!"

The warriors with Raldus bristled at the accusation, but he simply looked his father in the eyes and delivered his response with absolute calm.

"I tried to stop them. *We* tried. They will not listen. Not even the officers."

The elder warrior recognized the truth of this in his son's green eyes and inferred from the lines in his face and slumped shoulders how hard he'd struggled to contain the unfolding bloodlust. Though his rage still burned, he softened toward the young man standing before him and placed a hand upon his shoulder.

"There is nothing left for us here. The only honorable action remaining to us is to leave," he concluded, and Raldus nodded his assent. The warriors picked up their shields except for two who handed theirs to a friend before kneeling down to pick up the one bearing their fallen brother.

"What about them?" one warrior wondered aloud as he glanced around at the looting.

"These people no longer pose a danger to them, and the officers will restore order when the men have exhausted themselves," Mettius explained.

Raldus was already walking away, so the others followed, turning a blind eye and deaf ear to all who questioned them.

Chapter Twenty-Three

No Room For Fools

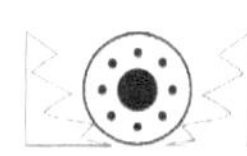

The two fully armored warriors strode down the colonnaded halls and marble floors of the senate building toward the debate chamber. All who saw the father/son duo quickly stepped out of their way with some going so far as to press themselves against the nearest wall to watch wide-eyed as Mettius and Raldus passed by.

They strode straight into the senate chamber, through the tunnel created by the two sides of the gallery seating, and into the center of the cavernous room facing the consul's dais. The only occupants were the consul himself and an aide taking up sheets of parchment as the overweight leader of the Naeran Republic signed and stamped them with his seal.

"There are the heroes of Naera!" the consul proclaimed after dismissing the aide with a wave and rising to his feet.

"Save your speeches," Mettius barked.

The consul took a step back as if to escape the forcefulness of the tone, and turned slightly away as he looked wide-eyed at Raldus for rescue, but the champion's face mirrored his father's fury.

"We fought to protect the republic and its people, not to turn it into a den of thieves and murderers," Raldus accused.

"What do you mean?" the consul questioned. Having recovered from the initial shock at this unexpected attitude, he reached out for the golden goblet on the small table beside his chair and took a sip of the wine.

"Your troops mercilessly massacred the residents of that city. They behaved like animals, and you are no better by not putting a stop to it even now," Mettius declared through gritted teeth.

"This is why you are upset?"

Both men nodded in the affirmative.

The consul chuckled and shook his head as he set his goblet down before stepping up to the front of the dais to look down at his guests.

"We have defeated an army of the gods! Why worry about exactly how it was done?"

"You still believe these people to be gods?" Raldus scoffed.

"There is no honor in the slaughter and looting of a defeated enemy," Mettius insisted.

"This is how we will become gods ourselves! Is it not glorious?"

Father and son looked at each other, and Mettius saw in his son's eyes the same sense of fatigue and defeat that now took hold of his own heart. There would be no reasoning with this man, and there could be no doubt the majority of the senators felt the same way given their vote to organize a task force to search the city for any sources of the powers they'd witnessed.

The two shared a nod, then returned their gaze to the consul whose flushed face beamed at them while he held one hand inside his toga with the other dangling at his side.

"I will rebuild Stoneforge and its warrior order, but we will not accept any contracts from this government. Our services will not be used to further your greed," Mettius concluded, then spun around and marched off without another word, his son right behind him.

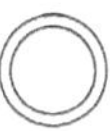

News had reached Keid days ago that the Stoneforge warriors left the battle for the city of Zaqulon while it was yet ongoing, but the reasons given for it proved to be nothing but conjecture and rumors. Most claimed that victory was inevitable, so the elite fighters decided their services were no longer necessary and left to attend to other matters. A few speculated that their code required it of them, but of course failed to explain why that might be.

One thing that Keid found intriguing was that amongst all the talk, he noticed that none dared accuse the warriors of cowardice. Was that borne from respect, or fear of reprisal?

When tidings came that Raldus had arrived in the city with the other warriors, Keid went to meet him only to be informed that the young man and his father had gone straight to the senate. The monk waited for them outside, but when they emerged and he saw their stormy visages, he chose not to approach.

He did not hear from his friend on that day, so when Raldus showed up at the monk's rented room, no longer armored and wearing only his belted white tunic and sandals, Keid eagerly welcomed him into the small space lit by a single, tiny window.

"What is it that has you so troubled, my friend? Please, tell me everything," Keid encouraged as they sat in the wooden chairs facing each other.

"Many of the things I have witnessed are not fit to be spoken, nor do I wish to burden you with such evil, but I will tell you what I can."

The warrior sighed as he stared at the floor, then told his story. He spoke of massive statues that issued forth fire from their eyes, the construction of grand weapons to knock them down, and of a stone city encircling a monumental crystal which glowed with an otherworldly light.

A single tear crept down Keid's cheek when Raldus revealed that Tullus was killed in the opening assault, then more followed and flowed freely when he explained about losing control of the army. The men turned feral, both the supposedly disciplined legionnaires of the republic and the fighters from Kostrai, slaughtering all within sight whether they fought back or not. This included men, women, and children; and when there was no one left to kill, they set about plundering all upon which they could lay their hands.

Only the Stoneforge Warriors restrained themselves from partaking in these activities, and once they were certain the enemy was no longer a threat, they left the battle and returned to republic lands alone.

When Raldus was finished, both warrior and monk stared at the floor in silence broken only by the chatter of passersby coming through the window from the street.

"It grieves me to learn of so many giving in to their hate and anger and inflicting so much death and suffering, but I also feel a sense of hope and peace to learn that all the members of your order denounced it and not just you."

"This is exactly what the code exists to prevent," Raldus despaired.

"Did you expect everyone to be living by *your* code?"

The young man looked up at the monk, the whites of his eyes standing out amid the shadows cast upon his face. His eyes grew distant as his focus turned inward upon the thoughts racing through his mind, and Keid waited patiently with his hands placed flat on his knees.

With a sigh, Raldus looked down and to the side before finally delivering his conclusion.

"I expected certain things to be understood by everyone, code or no code."

"You're not wrong. The scriptures tell us that all people are born with an ability to tell right from wrong, but it remains up to the individual to choose one or the other."

"I keep thinking that a year ago I would have done the exact same thing. Even now, with all I've learned and the vows I've made, I helped them do it."

"Nonsense!"

The monk leaned forward to ensure the weight of his words made it to his friend and remained that way until the young man met his gaze once more.

"You were an arrogant pup when I first met you, but even then I knew from the first moment we spoke that you are a man of honor who fights for the right reasons despite holding to misguided ambitions. Everything you did here was to protect your people, and you bear no fault in what others did as a result of the victory you helped obtain."

As they held each other's gaze, Keid saw pain and confusion within Raldus' green irises while from his own brown eyes he did his best to project sympathy and confidence.

"So there's nothing I can do about this?" Raldus questioned, revealing the true nature of his search for meaning.

"The only thing you can do is also the *best* thing you can do. Go home to your wife and daughter to be the husband and father they need while following our Lord Rosjen in all things," Keid admonished, then stood to indicate the visit was concluded.

Sighing, Raldus also stood up, nodded at the monk, and started toward the door only to stop and look back at the older man after a single step, his brow furrowed as he processed the wording and tone of the last thing he said.

"Aren't you coming with me?"

"My place is here. Some have shown they are willing to listen about Rosjen, and a few converted while you were away. I can't abandon them now."

"You're going to stay here alone?"

"I won't be alone. Rosjen is with us always, and once you tell the others of the seeds that are sprouting here, some of them will likely wish to join me. We may even be able to curb this hate and anger of which you have told me and stop the culture from becoming one of violence," Keid assured him.

Each man understood there was nothing more to be said, so they simply smiled at each other. Raldus nodded farewell as he left, having to turn partly sideways to fit his broad shoulders through the narrow door.

After he was gone, Keid whispered a short prayer asking for him to have safe travels and expressing his desire for them to see each other again in more peaceful times.

Chapter Twenty-Four

Welcome Home

There was little traffic on the snow-covered roads as Raldus journeyed home to Our Sacred Refuge with his father at his side. All of those who were displaced in the fighting were now back in their homes with whatever provisions they managed to gather before winter set in. Those few they did meet offered up gifts or pledged to sacrifice an animal on their behalf, but they politely declined these favors and rode on. They spoke little to each other, preferring to enjoy the silence of the season after all the chaos endured over the last year.

The other members of their order had returned to Stoneforge with the surviving townspeople to rebuild it, a task which Mettius expressed a great desire to be working on himself, but he agreed it could wait until after he met his son's wife and daughter.

After passing Fort Custonum, they encountered a group of Kostrai soldiers, one of the first to return home after helping to stabilize the borders. Each of these men wore their armor and weapons to make room for loot in the bulging sacks thrown over their shoulders.

These soldiers were too interested in their own war stories to even notice the warriors as they trotted past on their horses, but once they were out of earshot, father and son had something to say about them.

"Two nations have tasted the riches that come from destroying another. This can only lead to more war," Mettius griped.

"I fear you may be right, but this might also be as far as it goes. The republic has had the opportunity to completely destroy and loot Esbera many times, but has never done so," Raldus suggested.

"We shall see," Mettius concluded thoughtfully.

"At least the senate had enough good sense to lock away all the enemy weapons and armor," Raldus remarked, to which his father nodded in agreement.

Then a caravan of Naeran traders returning from Kostrai, carts laden with barrels of salted fish, spotted them and called out, so they put on their best polite smiles and slowed to speak with them.

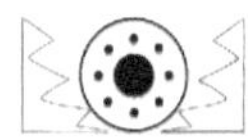

The stone arch previously described by his son came into view on the path ahead, so Mettius and Raldus dismounted their brown horses and held their reins to lead them the rest of the way. The white stallion which Raldus rode during the last months of the war he'd gifted to the eldest son of Legate Tullus in tribute to his father's memory.

They'd been alone ever since turning onto the forest path, which back in the city Raldus had described as narrow with spots of foliage growing upon it, but was now wide with the dirt packed down by multitudes of people and scarred with wheel tracks. As they neared the end of their journey, Mettius asked about this place which his son now called home and about this strange religion to which he now held.

The place sounded nice enough with its fertile farms and hospitable people, but the religion was pure nonsense. What sort of god sacrificed his own son for the sake of mortals?

Perhaps there was more to it that made it make sense, but Raldus only gave him the basics, which was all he was interested in anyway.

He personally paid homage to Malius, the god of heroes, as did most Stoneforge warriors, and didn't bother much with the beliefs of others. It wasn't productive to sit around all day guessing at mysteries beyond anyone's ability to comprehend.

Raldus led his horse through the arch first and Mettius followed close behind. On the other side, he saw his son handing the reins to a young boy in a wool shirt and pants and wearing leather shoes, and so did the same with his own reins.

The boy led the horses away and left the two of them standing there looking around at the stone brick plaza between hills with wooden buildings atop them.

"No welcoming party?" Mettius asked.

"They didn't know exactly when we would arrive. We should check in with the abbot," Raldus responded as he started toward the large building on their right.

"Abbot?"

"The leader of the monks, similar to a high priest."

An impressive set of stone stairs led from the plaza up to two large oak doors which they pushed open together to find themselves in a large room lit more by the roaring fire in the massive hearth to their right and torches on the walls than the sunlight filtering through the colored windows. A few grey-robed monks sitting on the benches facing the fireplace looked over at them and started whispering excitedly upon recognizing Raldus but did not rise to greet the two men.

Raldus led the way across a thick rug dominating the floor in the center of the room, under an interior balcony with a single staircase to their left, then through a door into a rear wing of the building. After that, he turned left and took them up a set of stairs and down a hallway to a single wood door beneath which could be seen flickering candlelight.

"Enter," a baritone voice responded to Raldus' single knock. The young man opened the door to reveal a spacious yet modestly furnished office. Behind the desk of solid wood sat a balding man with a white beard flowing over his grey robes, and behind him was a large window featuring a red circle on a blue background.

"Father, this is Abbot Jerald fodi Arilud. Abbot, this is my father, Mettius Velix," Raldus introduced once the two warriors were standing before the desk.

"Where is Keid?" Jerald immediately questioned, his voice heavy with suspicion.

"He chose to remain in the city ministering to new converts," Raldus responded.

"I should have known," Jerald grunted, then turned his attention to Mettius.

"So you are the one who taught this boy a life of violence?"

"I taught him to defend himself and others," Mettius growled.

"You taught him to kill."

"Only when necessary."

"Who decides when it is necessary?"

"If you have something to say; say it," Mettius demanded as he crossed his arms over his chest.

"A man who seeks out death and teaches others to do the same is not to be trusted."

"Death comes to us all, and few get to choose the manner in which it comes. A man who fails to recognize that and fight to preserve life is not to be respected."

Both men fell silent as they glared at each other, neither willing to admit the other might have a point.

Several seconds passed, then Raldus broke the silence by clearing his throat, drawing the attention of those who'd forgotten he was there.

"I came to inform you that I've returned and to confirm that we are safe," he interjected.

"For now," Mettius and Jerald said at the same time. Their eyes met again, and in the monk's brown eyes the warrior noted a trace of begrudging respect which he also felt.

Of course, neither of them were going to admit that any time soon.

Satisfied that her baby was fed and properly burped, Ariela laid her in the cradle in a corner of the kitchen, then set to work preparing the noonday meal for her father, brother, and herself.

The men should be out in the barns for at least another hour, but she'd just finished chopping the dried vegetables when she heard the door open and someone come in. She glanced at the baby to make sure the sound hadn't woken her, then headed to the front room while wiping her hands on her apron.

When she rounded the corner, she froze with both hands wrapped in the apron upon seeing two muscular men in Naeran tunics standing by the now closed door looking at her.

"You're home," she breathed, finally letting go of her apron as she walked up to her husband who wrapped her up in his strong arms.

"Are you well," he whispered into her ear, and she responded with a few short nods that rubbed their cheeks together.

With that, he let her go, and she stepped back to look at the other man who looked much like an older version of her husband.

"This is my father, Mettius."

"Welcome to our home," she greeted as she bowed her head toward him.

"I'm pleased to meet you," Mettius responded, his voice rough from many years of shouted commands.

"Is she here?" Raldus questioned impatiently.

"Quietly now. She's sleeping," Ariela cautioned as she turned to lead them into the kitchen.

She indicated the cradle with a nod, then stood back with her husband's father to give Raldus space to gaze upon his child for the first time. He tiptoed up to the cradle, his steps sure and silent from great experience in sneaking around, and leaned over to gaze upon the chubby face peeking out from the blanket wrapped around her.

"What's her name?" he asked, his whisper scarcely audible on the other side of the room.

"Frida Velix."

Though he was turned away from her, Ariela saw his ears twitch from the soft smile she knew had formed on his face upon hearing his name with that of his child's.

He stayed that way for a while, then turned to look at his father, who accepted the invite and went up beside his son to view his granddaughter.

Ariela marveled at the sight of two rough men turned into mush at the sight of a baby, then returned to the counter to resume preparing the meal. They still had to eat, after all.

"You have learned what we believe, but do not seem to care," Jerald challenged the elder warrior.

"That's because I don't," Mettius admitted.

"Why?"

"Why would I?"

"Why do you resist answering?"

"Why do you?"

The abbot silently groaned, careful not to give his opponent the satisfaction of having frustrated him, but chose to drop the subject.

"How long do you plan to stay?"

"Not long. I wanted to meet the new members of my family and the community in which my son now resides, but I have much work to do."

"Such as?"

The warrior gave him a narrow-eyed glance without any interruption to his stride on the path circling the farms. Normally, Jerald didn't like to drag his weary bones down the steps from the monastery, but after nearly three weeks of this man's stubborn refusal to respond to the teachings of his monks, he'd decided it was time to seek him out.

At least the weather was relatively warm today with the first signs of the coming spring so his joints weren't aching near as bad as in the previous weeks, but that also meant having to walk in mud thanks to the melting snow.

"Rebuilding our town and the warrior order," Mettius finally answered after returning his gaze forward.

"It is my understanding that the reason your order exists is to provide for a town that cannot grow its own food. Perhaps it is time to relocate?"

"I suppose you're about to suggest we all come here and convert to your religion?"

"I'm not fond of the idea of more outsiders coming to live here, but it is an option. As for converting, that choice is for the individual to make. We do not force anyone to accept our beliefs as their own."

Neither spoke for a time. The sounds of splitting logs, the bleating of sheep and lowing of cattle, and the occasional shout of a farm worker accompanied them as they rounded the north end of the fields by the main barn and pond beside it.

"That may be how it started, but now it is our home and way of life," Mettius finally explained.

"Is that any reason to go on killing, and being killed?"

"Again with the killing! Look, it comes down to one thing. There will always be people in this world who harm others out of self-interest, not to mention wild animals that go after livestock and children, and someone must stand between them and the good people merely trying to live their lives."

Now it was Jerald's turn to be silent. He hated to admit it, but there was truth in the man's words. Where would any of them be now if men of violence hadn't stood against the evils seen in the last two years?

"Will Raldus be returning with you?" he asked, choosing to change the subject rather than continue an endless debate.

"That will be his choice."

Raldus gave the horse one last good brush, then stepped back and ran an arm across his forehead as he glanced over the shiny brown coat to make sure he hadn't missed any spots.

He exited the stall, closed the gate, and turned to see his wife's father, Imri, standing in the middle of the barn watching him.

"I've been meaning to talk with you," Raldus remarked as he passed him on his way to hang the brush from a hook on the wall.

"I gathered as much," Imri replied solemnly.

Sighing, Raldus turned away from the wall to address his next statement to the man's face.

"I've decided to return to Stoneforge with my father. I need to do my part in rebuilding my home."

"*This* is your home now."

"That doesn't change my responsibility to the place of my birth," Raldus insisted.

Imri indicated his understanding with a short nod.

"I'll tell Ariela tonight. When I reach Naera, I'll hire a courier service to come once a month to see that all is well," Raldus revealed, then started to walk away.

"You aren't taking her with you?" Imri questioned.

"No. I will not take her from her home and family, and this is still the safest place I know," he answered without stopping, then was out the door before any more questions could be asked.

"How long will you be gone?" Ariela asked, struggling to speak through the tightness gripping her throat and chest. Her husband had been home less than a month and now he was talking about leaving her again.

"I don't know. It'll probably take years to rebuild the town, and even longer to restore the order," Raldus admitted, looking down and to the side as he spoke.

"You marry me, father a child with me, leave to fight a war, and now you intend to be gone for however many years?"

"I'll visit every chance I get," he promised while continuing to avoid her gaze.

She could do nothing but stare at him and wonder what kind of man she had married that would abandon his family so easily. Angry tears burned at the corners of her eyes as she looked away toward the cradle in the center of the main room where Baby Frida quietly fussed.

"Why?" she croaked out.

"I abandoned my people once, and can't do it again in their time of greatest need. The only thing I want more than to be with you is for you to be safe, and this is the safest place I know," he explained, his own voice strained from emotion.

Her eyes went wide as she looked at him again, and she silently chastised herself for being a fool. She should have known he was just being overprotective as always.

"I'm going with you," she declared.

His head shot up and eyes locked with hers.

"No! It is better for you and Frida to stay here with your family," he argued.

"The *only* place for me is with my husband and hers is with both of her parents!" she shot back.

"It isn't safe!"

"How?! How is it not safe? Haven't the invaders been driven off, and the bandits from last year all been defeated?"

"There's no way to know what might happen."

"That's life."

His mouth opened and closed as he tried to find a way to argue with that. Meanwhile, she stared at him with her head cocked to one side daring him to say something foolish.

The door opened before either spoke again, and they turned to see her father and brother entering.

"We're coming too," Imri declared. She looked at her brother, who glanced away but not before she spotted the redness on his face and neck which revealed that they must have been listening for some time.

"My inte*nt is* to not uproot you from your home. Certainly not for my sake," Raldus insisted.

"You are family now, and Ariela is right. A wife belongs with her husband, and I'm not ready to part from my daughter and granddaughter," Imri explained.

"You've never left this place before."

"Times are changing, and our isolation is ending, whether we want it to or not. I may be an old man, but I'm not so set in my ways that I can't recognize the way the wind is blowing and make a choice to follow it."

When she looked back at Raldus, Ariela saw the familiar stubbornness hardening his eyes and spoke up before he continued arguing.

"This is our decision. We are going to Stoneforge, even if we have to follow on our own after you leave. You know I'll do it. Isn't it better that we all go together?"

He met her gaze, and his green eyes gradually softened as he looked into hers.

"There's a chance we'll never come back here," he warned.

"We understand," Imri assured him from behind Ariela.

"So be it."

The cart purchased from a nearby village was too big to fit through the arch granting entrance through the stone wall surrounding the monastery and town, so it had to be loaded beside the forest path. That task was now finished, Ariela was seated comfortably on the driver's bench cradling Frida in her arms, and Imri sat next to her with the reins for the single mule in his hands. Raldus and Mettius were each astride the horse upon which they'd arrived a month earlier and were initially loaned to them by the army. The town couldn't spare any other horses, so Tobias remained on foot beside the cart near his older sister.

Raldus smiled at his wife, then pulled his horse around to take one last look at the bearded old man watching them from under the arch. Jerald raised his right hand in farewell, which Raldus acknowledged with a nod, while behind him Tobias also returned the wave.

He turned back toward the path, nodded once at his father, then spurred his beast forward.

Time for another adventure.

Hopefully a peaceful one this time.

Find more from this author on Amazon!

Acknowledgements

Thank you to my dad for his continued support and encouragement on this never-ending journey of mine.

Special thanks to Amanda Collins and Gabriel Garcia for their feedback in the drafting stages.

And to all my friends who tolerate my rambling on about non-existent worlds and my constant requests for feedback.

About the author

Dodge Merrin writes character-driven speculative fiction that explores what people believe and why they fight for it. His work spans military science fiction, epic fantasy, and paranormal adventure united by morally complex characters, multiple perspectives, and stories that ask difficult questions about right, wrong, and everything in between.

He creates worlds where both sides of conflict have noble goals, where heroes make terrible choices for good reasons, and where no one's hands stay clean. His books challenge readers to question their assumptions about heroes, villains, and the nature of conflict itself.

When not immersed in the fictional worlds he creates, Dodge lives in southern Missouri with his two cats, Merry and Pippin, who provide equal parts comfort, chaos, and inspiration for his work.

Also by Dodge Merrin

Follow me on Amazon!

Rising Shadows Trilogy

Echoes of Darkness

Available through Amazon & KU. https://mybook.to/echoesofdarkness

Night Comes Again

Available through Amazon. https://mybook.to/nightcomesagain

Suffer No Evil

Available through Amazon https://mybook.to/suffernoevil

Embers of Hope Science Fiction Miniseries

Triumphant Empire

Available through Amazon & KU. https://mybook.to/faRL1

Revolution

Available through Amazon. https://mybook.to/cNVFXJ

Total War

Available through Amazon. https://mybook.to/7Ph2

Brink of Extinction

Available through Amazon. https://mybook.to/CeUCF

See Also

Humble Glory

Available through Amazon & KU. https://mybook.to/H4ePYWh

www.ingramcontent.com/pod-product-compliance
Lightning Source LLC
LaVergne TN
LVHW090600110826
845146LV00001B/196
* 9 7 9 8 9 9 5 2 5 9 9 0 9 *